JESSI'S B

"If Aunt Cec b... ere a good ...ore
she'd trust ...da... ...pa...s tr...
they set ... ...ut they do tr...
me use ...en and coo... 29 JAN 2001
choose ...n clothes. N...
shop ...nce we have th...
us ...de what to wear t... ...a
restaurant or wherever we ...e goi... ...unt
Cecelia oesn't trust us to do ...ning
right."

I felt ...iserable. I know ...looked miserable.
This was because Dawn said, "You look *so*
miserable, essi."

"Boy," I replied. "If I ...ids of my own,
I'm *never* going to treat them the way Aunt
Dictator treats Becca, Squirt and me."

Oh no! With both their parents working,
the Ramsey kids have got a new babysitter
—the dreaded Aunt Cecelia. Jessi knows
she doesn't need a babysitter, she is one!
But will her aunt *ever* learn to trust her.

Also in the Babysitters Club series:

Kristy's Great Idea
Claudia and the Phantom Phone Calls
The Truth About Stacey
Mary Anne Saves the Day
Dawn and the Impossible Three
Kristy's Big Day
Claudia and Mean Janine
Boy-Crazy Stacey
The Ghost at Dawn's House
Logan Likes Mary Anne!
Kristy and the Snobs
Claudia and the New Girl
Goodbye Stacey, Goodbye
Hello, Mallory
Little Miss Stoneybrook . . . and Dawn
Jessi's Secret Language
Mary Anne's Bad-Luck Mystery
Stacey's Mistake
Claudia and the Bad Joke
Kristy and the Walking Disaster
Mallory and the Trouble with Twins
Jessi Ramsey, Pet-Sitter
Dawn on the Coast
Kristy and the Mother's Day Surprise
Mary Anne and the Search for Tigger
Claudia and the Sad Goodbye
Jessi and the Superbrat
Welcome Back, Stacey!
Mallory and the Mystery Diary
Mary Anne and the Great Romance
Dawn's Wicked Stepsister
Kristy and the Secret of Susan
Claudia and the Great Search
Mary Anne and Too Many Boys
Stacey and the Mystery of Stoneybrook

Look out for:
Dawn and the Older Boy
Kristy and the Mystery Admirer
Poor Mallory!
Claudia and the Middle School Mystery

Babysitters' Specials:
Babysitters on Board!
Babysitters' Summer Holiday
Babysitters' Winter Holiday
Babysitters' Island Adventure
California Girls
New York, New York!
Snowbound

JESSI'S BABYSITTER

Ann M. Martin

Hippo Books
Scholastic Children's Books
London

Scholastic Children's Books,
Scholastic Publications Ltd,
7–9 Pratt Street, London NW1 0AE, UK

Scholastic Inc.,
730 Broadway, New York, NY 10003, USA

Scholastic Canada Ltd,
123 Newkirk Road, Richmond Hill,
Ontario, Canada L4C 3G5

Ashton Scholastic Pty Ltd,
P O Box 579, Gosford, New South Wales,
Australia

Ashton Scholastic Ltd,
Private Bag 1, Penrose, Auckland,
New Zealand

First published in the US by Scholastic Inc., 1990
First published in the UK by Scholastic Publications Ltd, 1993

Text copyright © Ann M. Martin, 1990
THE BABYSITTERS CLUB is a registered trademark of Scholastic Inc.

ISBN 0 590 55145 0

Typeset in Plantin by Contour Typesetters, Southall, London
Printed by Cox & Wyman Ltd, Reading, Berks.

10 9 8 7 6 5 4 3 2 1

*This book is dedicated
to the memory of
Eugene Dougherty,
who taught me how to
make writing exciting.*

1st CHAPTER

"*Plié* first pozeetion, *plié* second pozeetion —nice and slowly—*plié* sird pozeetion, *plié* fourse pozeetion—*veeerry* slowly—*plié* fifs pozeetion . . . and . . . stop. . . . Non, non, non!" cried Madame Noelle. "Do not fall to zee floor. Come to a nice, graceful stop like zee lovely ballerinas you are. Now, once again."

We *pliéed* in all the pozeetions again and then came to a nice, graceful stop, even though I—and every other pupil in my class—just wanted to lie down and sleep for a week. We had been working hard.

I am Jessica Ramsey, otherwise known as Jessi. I am eleven years old. I'm in the sixth grade at Stoneybrook Middle School (SMS). In case you can't tell, I am also a dancer. (Or as Madame Noelle would say, a doncer.) I live in Stoneybrook, Connecticut, but I have ballet lessons at a special school

1

in Stamford, another Connecticut town (actually, a city), which isn't too far from home.

Ballet is a very important part of my life. Maybe I'll go to a dance school in New York City. Maybe I'll even become a professional dancer.

Class ended that day when my friends and I didn't keel over after the last round of pliés. We changed out of our toe shoes (I am proud to say that I can dance *en pointe*), and slipped jeans or skirts over our leotards. Then we waited for our parents to pick us up.

Usually my mum comes to get me, but that day I waited and waited. Finally, fifteen minutes after everyone else had left, my dad drove up. He works in Stamford, but my lessons usually end long before he's ready to leave the office.

I ran to his car.

"Daddy!" I cried. "How come *you're* picking me up? Where's Mama? Has something happened to Becca or Squirt?"

Becca is my younger sister. She's eight. Squirt is my baby brother. His real name is John Philip Ramsey, Jr., but since he was the smallest baby in the hospital when he was born, the nurses started calling him Squirt. And the name stuck, even though now Squirt is the same size as most other toddlers his age.

Daddy smiled at me. "Don't worry," he

said, as I slid into the front seat of the car. "Everyone's fine. I decided to leave work early today, so I phoned your mother and told her I'd bring you home. It would be silly for her to make the trip when I'm already here."

"Why'd you leave early?" I wanted to know. And just then a smell (well, not a smell; a wonderful chocolaty aroma) drifted to me. I turned round and saw a white cake box on the back seat. "Hey, what's that?"

"You're certainly full of questions today," remarked Daddy. "Let's see. I left early because we have something to celebrate tonight, and the box on the back seat is part of the celebration."

"A celebration? Oh, goody!" I cried, reaching for the box.

"No peeking," said Daddy.

"But I want to see what's in there."

"The celebration is a surprise. You'll find out all about it after dinner."

I couldn't help guessing. "You've been promoted!" I exclaimed.

Daddy shook his head.

"You've got a pay rise."

"Nope."

"We're moving back to New Jersey?"

I wasn't quite as excited by that idea. The funny thing is, a few months ago, I would have jumped at the chance to leave Stoneybrook and return to Oakley, New Jersey, the town in which I grew up. My family and I had been happy there. We are black, and our neighbourhood, school, and even my ballet school in Oakley were all mixed up— black people and white people, living and working together. Also, my relatives lived nearby. One of my cousins, Keisha, was my best friend. When Daddy's company offered him a better job in Stamford, he jumped at the chance. But it meant we had to move. I didn't want to leave Oakley. But I wasn't prepared for what would greet us in Stoneybrook—prejudice, that's what. We moved to a town with only a few black residents. I am the only black pupil in the entire sixth grade. People teased my family. People said nasty things to us. People ignored us.

At first.

Slowly, though, a change came about. I made some friends. They became good friends. Becca and I each made a best friend. Now I can't imagine going back to Oakley. I'd have to leave too many memories behind—like my babysitting adventures. Or the time our whole school went on a trip to a ski lodge in Vermont. Or the time my friends and I went to summer camp.

But luckily Daddy said, "No, we're not moving."

Then it hit me. "You're having a baby, aren't you? You and Mama are having a *ba*by! Oh, I hope it's another boy. Then our family would be even. Two girls, two boys."

4

Daddy chuckled. "It's not a new baby, either," he said. "And why don't you stop guessing? I'm afraid I'll give it away if you really do guess it."

"Okay," I said, but I continued guessing in my head. We'd won the lottery. We were going on a trip to Disney World—or maybe even Texas. I had always wanted to see Texas. Then I got another idea. I bet Mama and Daddy really were having a baby, but Daddy was too clever to let on.

All the way to Stoneybrook, I hugged the secret to myself. As soon as Daddy parked the car in the drive, I ran inside and straight up to Becca's room.

"Guess what! Guess what!" I cried.

Becca looked up from her third-grade homework. "What?"

"Daddy's brought a cake home and he says we're celebrating something tonight, but he won't say what. You know what I think, though? I think Mama and Daddy are going to have another baby!"

"You *do*?" Becca's eyes widened.

"Yup. I really do."

I was wrong. After dinner that evening, Daddy brought out the cake. When he had cut it and served it, he said, "We have something wonderful to celebrate."

I glanced at Becca. She glanced back, trying not to smile.

"Your mother—" Daddy began.

"I knew it! I knew it!" I cried.

"You knew that your mother's found a job?" Daddy asked me.

"I—I—Mama's got a job?" I repeated.

Mama was grinning away at the end of the dining room table. "That's right," she said. It's time for me to go back to work. I was in advertising before you girls were born, and at last I can go back to that. I'm really looking forward to it. My job starts on Monday. Five days a week. Nine to five, probably longer days every now and then."

Becca and I knew how important this was to Mama, so we cheered, jumped up from our places at the table, and ran to hug her.

Then I said, settling down again, "Boy, I suppose you'll really need me to babysit now. I'll take care of Becca and Squirt every afternoon that I can. But who will look after Squirt while I'm at school? And who will babysit while I'm at my dance lessons? And, hey! Who will *drive* me to my ballet class?"

Mama and Daddy exchanged a look. I didn't like the look of it.

"What?" I asked. "What is it?"

"Well," Daddy began, and cleared his throat, "your mother will need more than just a sitter. She won't have time to shop or cook or do the housework. So . . . um . . . so your Aunt Cecelia is going to move in. In a couple of weeks."

"Aunt Cecelia!" cried Becca and I at the same time. "Nooo!"

Aunt Cecelia is absolutely awful. I can't tell you how many things are wrong with her. She may be Daddy's older sister, but she smells funny. Bad perfume, probably. And she's bossy and mean and thinks Mama and Daddy aren't bringing up Becca and Squirt and me properly. She thinks they let us run wild, which couldn't be further from the truth. What happened was that not long ago, Mama and Daddy went away on a three-day weekend. They left me in charge, since we had a mini-holiday from school. It was the first time I'd been allowed to babysit overnight. Unfortunately, Becca had been invited to go sailing on Saturday— and the boats got caught in a storm, and Becca and the others were stranded on an island off the coast of Connecticut for two days. No one knew where they were. Aunt Cecelia came to stay until the crisis was over, and she was appalled that Mama and Daddy had left me in charge of Becca and Squirt.

She thought something was seriously wrong with our family.

I think she also wanted a family to live with, since her husband had died recently, and she was all alone in the house she'd moved to in Queenstown, Connecticut. After that she found that she couldn't bear to stay in her home in Oakley. The house had too many memories.

This is my Aunt Cecelia: bossy, strict, mean.

Becca and I cannot stand her. And now she would be *living* with us. She would be caring for Squirt, cooking, and helping with the housework. She would also be . . . my babysitter. I'm far too old and responsible to need a babysitter. After all, I'm a sitter myself.

But Aunt Cecelia doesn't trust me. She thinks it was my fault that Becca got lost at sea, even though Mama and Daddy gave Becca permission to go on the sailing trip.

When the "celebration" was over, Becca and I huddled in my room.

"Can you *believe* this?" I asked her. "Aunt Cecelia coming here. Moving *in*. This is a nightmare."

"A triple nightmare," agreed Becca. "Maybe we could talk Mama and Daddy out of letting her come."

"I don't think so," I said. "But I bet we could fix it so that Aunt Cecelia wouldn't want to stay once she got here. You know, put shaving cream in her slippers, a fake spider on her pillow."

"Honey in her hairbrush!" cried Becca.

"Shh!" I hissed. "That's a great idea, but keep your voice down. We don't want Mama and Daddy to know what we're up to."

2nd CHAPTER

Becca and I plotted about a dozen ways to get Aunt Cecelia to leave. Most of them were very mean. We wrote them on a list, which I hid way back in my desk drawer.

Then Becca left.

I sat on my bed and felt depressed for a while. Then I did what I always do in a tough situation.

I called my best friend, Mallory Pike.

Ring, ring went the Pikes' phone.

"Hello?" said a voice. It was Nicky, Mal's brother. (Mal has *seven* younger brothers and sisters.)

"Hi, Nicky. It's Jessi. Is Mal home?"

"Yup."

"Well, can I speak to her, please?"

"Maybe."

"*Nicky.*"

"Okay, okay, okay. . . . Oh, wait a second. I've just remembered. Mal isn't here after all. She went to the shops with Mum."

"Could you ask her to call me back, please?" I asked. "I really need to talk to her. This is a matter of life and death . . . sort of."

"Life and death?" repeated Nicky. "Gosh."

We got off the phone. I went back to my room. I closed the door. Then I opened my door again and hung a sign on it that I'd made. The sign read (in big bold letters):

KEEP OUT (please)
THIS MEANS YOU
PRIVACY NEEDED
(THANK YOU FOR YOUR COOPERATION)

Mallory thinks the sign is silly. She says that if you want people to stay out of your room, you should put up a sign that just says: STAY OUT OR ELSE.

I think one reason Mal is my best friend is because I like her family. The Pikes are very open and relaxed. There aren't too many rules in the Pike house, even though there are a lot of kids. Here's who's in Mal's family, besides Mal and her parents: Byron, Adam, and Jordan, who are *identical triplets* (they're ten years old); Vanessa, who's nine, very dreamy, and wants to be a poet; Nicky, who's eight, and gets pushed around by his big brothers; Margo, who's seven, and likes to tease; and Claire, who's five, the baby of the family, and seems to be stuck in a silly stage. She calls everybody "silly-billy-goo-goo".

At the Pikes', something is always going on. With eight kids, I suppose that's not surprising. Anyway, Mal's household certainly is different from mine. Even so, Mallory and I are alike in many ways. We're both the oldest in our families, but we feel that our parents won't let us grow up fast enough. We practically had to kick and scream in order to be allowed to get our ears pierced. Then Mal, who wears glasses, asked if she could have contact lenses, but her parents said no. They think she's too young. (Furthermore, Mal now has a brace, so she isn't feeling particularly pretty these days, despite her pierced ears.) As for me, well, talk about being treated like a baby. Now Aunt Cecelia was going to move in. I would have a *baby*sitter—and I'm a sitter myself!

Mal and I also have some good things in common. We both love reading. Our favourite books are horse stories, especially the ones by Marguerite Henry, such as *Misty of Chincoteague* and *Stormy, Misty's Foal*. Mal likes to write, too. She's kept a journal for years and recently talked me into keeping one as well.

However, we do have our differences. As

you know, I want to be a ballerina one day (I think), but Mal wants to be an author and illustrator of children's books. The other difference is pretty obvious, I suppose— our looks. Mal is white, with red hair and freckles, and she's about average height. I'm black, with long eyelashes (Mama is jealous of them) and long, *long* legs. I'm lucky to have those legs for dancing.

I'm also lucky to have found a best friend in Stoneybrook, especially after leaving Keisha behind in Oakley, but I feel even luckier to have made other friends as well. It's always nice to have a group of friends, I thought, as I settled down for a good daydream. And my group of friends are the members of the Babysitters Club.

I suppose I haven't mentioned the BSC yet, have I? Well, the BSC consists of seven girls who have a business doing babysitting in our neighbourhoods. We meet three times a week and get lots of sitting jobs. Mal and I are both members—junior officers. We feel honoured to be part of the club, because the other members are all thirteen-year-old eighth-graders.

Kristy Thomas is the club chairman. Her family is as big as the Pikes', but it's much more complicated. Let's see. How do I even begin to tell you about her family? I suppose I should start a year or so ago when Kristy was living in Bradford Court in the house she'd grown up in. She lived with her mum;

her older brothers, Sam and Charlie; and her little brother, David Michael. Her father walked out on her family not long after David Michael was born. Kristy rarely heard from him. (She still doesn't.) Anyway, the summer after the seventh grade, Kristy's mum married this man she'd been going out with. His name is Watson Brewer and he's a millionaire. Honestly. Watson moved Kristy's family into his mansion across town. That was when things began getting confusing. Watson has two children (Karen, who's seven, and Andrew, who's four) from his first marriage. Karen and Andrew live with their father every other weekend. Then, not long ago, the Brewers adopted Emily Michelle, a two-year-old Vietnamese girl. And *then*, Nannie, Kristy's grandmother, moved in to help take care of Emily Michelle. (Nannie is not a bit like Aunt Cecelia. She's nice.) The Brewers also have a dog and a cat.

Kristy is nice but bossy. She's a tomboy, and she coaches a team of little kids who like to play softball. She's *full* of ideas. (She started the Babysitters Club.) Kristy is also a bit immature compared to her friends. She's not very interested in clothes yet, she *never* wears make-up, and she doesn't iike boys particularly. But she does like a boy in her neighbourhood! His name is Bart and he's very nice.

Kristy's best friend is Mary Anne Spier,

the secretary of the club. Kristy and Mary Anne are similar to Mal and me in that they're very alike in some ways and very different in others. For one thing, they look a little alike. They both have brown eyes and brown hair and are short. (Kristy is shorter.) And Mary Anne used to dress in a babyish way, but now she cares much more about clothes than she used to. I think the similarities end there. Mary Anne is quiet and shy—although she's the only one of us to have a steady boyfriend. Her boyfriend is Logan Bruno, and he's actually part of the BSC, but I'll explain how later. Mary Anne's family used to be as different from Kristy's as you could imagine, but now it has changed. Mary Anne's mum died when Mary Anne was really little, so Mary Anne grew up an only child living with her dad, who was quite strict. Then Mr Spier met an old high-school girlfriend of his (who was divorced by then), and after a pretty long time, they finally got married. Guess who the girlfriend was—the mother of Dawn Schafer, another club member, and Mary Anne's other best friend. Dawn, her brother, and her mum had moved back to Stoney-brook (they'd been living in California) after the Schafers' divorce. Dawn and Mary Anne became friends, then their parents began going out together, and now the best friends are stepsisters, too. They all live in Dawn's house, which is a colonial farmhouse.

Dawn is *so* cool. (Or, as Claudia Kishi, another BSC member, would say, she's *fresh*.) Dawn has long pale blonde hair that reaches halfway down her back. Her eyes are sparkling blue. She dresses in a casual style all her own. And, although she likes Stoneybrook and her new family, she longs for California—for a couple of reasons. In the first place, she was brought up there. She misses the house she grew up in, the warmer climate, and of course, her father. She also misses her brother. That's right. Jeff is back in California, living with Mr Schafer. He just never adjusted to Connecticut the way Dawn did. He had trouble at school and he wasn't happy. So he returned to California. At first Dawn felt terrible. She felt as if her family had been ripped in two. Now that she's got a stepfather and a stepsister (not to mention a kitten—Mary Anne's), she feels more complete. But she still visits her father and Jeff whenever she can.

Things at the Schafer/Spier home got off to a troubled start after the wedding. Dawn and Mary Anne were friends, but they weren't prepared to be stepsisters. And Dawn and her mum are as different from Mary Anne and her dad as night and day. They have varying ideas on everything from meals to housecleaning. But they're overcoming things. I think that deep down,

Dawn and Mary Anne are happy to be step-sisters.

Let's see. The two remaining BSC members are Claudia Kishi, club vice-chairman, and Stacey McGill, club treasurer. Claudia and Stacey are best friends and also have their similarities and differences. (I suppose all best friends do.) Both Claudia and Stacey are pretty *fresh* themselves. They are the most sophisticated of all us members. None of us really comes straight out and says that, but we all know it's true.

Claudia comes from a pretty normal family. It's like mine, I suppose. She lives with her parents and her older sister, Janine. Janine, however, is a genius in the true sense of the word (she has an amazingly high I.Q.), while Claudia, who's bright, is a terrible pupil. She just doesn't like school. (Oh, and she's an awful speller.) What she does like is art, and she's really talented. Claud can sculpt, paint, draw, you name it. She even makes wild jewellery to go with her wild clothes. Claud wears things my mother won't even let me *look* at in shops— short, short skirts and tight black trousers and off-the-shoulder sweat shirts. Also, she can think of a thousand ways to wear her hair, which is long, silky, and jet-black. Claud is Japanese-American and very exotic-looking. She's also good fun. She loves reading Nancy Drew mysteries and eating junk food, but her parents don't approve of either habit. Does that deter Claudia? No. She just hides the books and food all round her room. Once, I dropped a pencil on the floor and it rolled under an armchair. I reached down to pick it up, and my hand closed over a Yorkie Bar! Claud likes boys and goes out on dates and to school dances, but she doesn't have one special boyfriend yet. There's one sad thing about Claudia. Her grandmother, Mimi, used to live with her family. I think Claudia was closer to Mimi than to anyone else in the world. Then Mimi got ill and died. That was a hard time for all of us, but especially for Claud.

And now we come to Stacey. Stacey shares Claudia's sense of fashion and, if this is possible, she's even more sophisticated than Claud. Her mother lets her perm her hair, she has pierced ears (well, so do all of us, except for Kristy and Mary Anne), and her clothes are even more cool than Claudia's. I think. Actually, maybe they're about equal on the coolness scale.

But there's one thing about Stacey that none of us can top: she grew up in New York City. Big, thrilling, exciting New York City, the shopping capital of the world. How did Stacey end up in Stoneybrook? Well, the company Mr McGill works for transferred his job to Stamford, so Stacey and her parents settled in Stoneybrook. (Stacey's an only child.) Then, after they'd been here about a year, Mr McGill was transferred *back* to New York. (When they left, they sold their house—to my family!) Anyway, that was when the trouble started. Mr and Mrs McGill began having problems. Finally, they separated. Mrs McGill wanted to move back here, while Mr McGill stayed in the city. It was a tough decision, but Stacey finally chose to live with her mum in Stoneybrook. (Boy, were we glad to have her back.) So Stacey's life might seem glamorous, but it hasn't been easy. Especially when you consider that on top of everything else, Stacey has a disease called diabetes. She has to stay on a strict no-sweets diet and give herself daily injections of something called insulin (Ugh!) All in all, though, Stacey copes pretty well, even when she isn't feeling too great. And she's a very good friend to all of us.

The phone rang then, and it jolted me out of my daydream. I jumped off my bed. I hadn't begun my homework. I hadn't practised at my *barre* in the basement, either. Even so, I hoped the phone call was from Mallory. Homework or not, practice or not, all I wanted to do was pour out the story of Aunt Cecelia to my best friend.

3rd CHAPTER

"'Bye, Mama!" I called. "I'm going to Claudia's for the meeting. I'll be back in time for dinner!"

"Have fun, darling," my mother replied.

I dashed into our garage, hopped onto my bike, and cycled towards Claud's house, hurrying. It's never a good idea to be late for a meeting. Kristy feels it is her duty as chairman to run the BSC meetings in as official a manner as possible. So I pedalled along quickly.

On the way I thought about how nice it was having Mama at home. I'd never thought about it before; I suppose because there was no reason to think of her *not* being there. Even when she began to job-hunt, I didn't think what it would be like to have two working parents. It didn't seem real enough.

But now that Mama would soon *not* be at

home, I spent a good deal of time appreciating having her around. It was nice to get in from school and find her in the study, paying bills; or on the phone, doing voluntary work; or best of all, in the kitchen, baking, with Squirt at her heels. Soon all that would be over. I'd come home to . . . Aunt Cecelia. (I always imagined scary music playing when I thought of her name.) And when I left for a club meeting, I would have to call goodbye to . . . Aunt Cecelia.

My own babysitter.

I pulled into Claud's drive and chained my bike to a lamppost. Then I let myself into the Kishis' house. There's no point in ringing the bell, because both Mr and Mrs Kishi work, and Janine isn't often at home, so all us club members just run upstairs instead of making Claudia come downstairs when we know perfectly well where to go.

"Hi!" I said, entering Claud's room.

Claudia, Kristy, and Dawn were there, in their usual places. I took *my* usual place.

"Hi, Jessi!" my friends replied.

Claud and Dawn were sitting on Claud's bed, leaning against the wall. Kristy was perched in the director's chair, which she has claimed as her own—the chairman's throne. She was wearing a visor, and a pencil was stuck over one ear.

I sat on the floor. We were waiting for Mallory, Stacey, and Mary Anne. While we waited, I only half listened to the others, who were talking loudly. I couldn't help thinking about Aunt Cecelia, about how Mama and Daddy had got me a *babysitter*. And then I began to think about our own sitting club.

This is how the BSC got started. It all began more than a year ago, when Kristy, Claudia, Mary Anne, and Stacey were new seventh-grade students at SMS. I still lived in New Jersey then, Dawn still lived in California, and Mal was a lowly fifth-grader at Stoneybrook Elementary. She wasn't even a sitter yet.

Anyway, back then, Kristy lived across the street from Claud, and Mary Anne lived next door to her. All three of them had grown up together and all liked to babysit, but they did their sitting on their own. Then one day Kristy's mum (who was just beginning to see Watson Brewer) needed a sitter for David Michael, who was only six. No one was available—not Kristy, not Sam or Charlie, not any of the sitters Mrs Thomas had phoned. It was while Kristy was watching her mother make all those telephone calls that she got what was probably the most brilliant idea of her life. Wouldn't it be easy if her mum could make just *one* phone call and reach a lot of sitters at once? Of course it would!

So she told Claudia and Mary Anne about her idea for a sitting business, and they formed the Babysitters Club. They asked Stacey to join, too. She and Claud were already getting to be friends, and the girls thought that four sitters would be better than three. That was the start of the BSC.

The club did well from the beginning, thanks partly to all the advertising the girls did and partly to the fact that they were (and still are) excellent sitters, so people asked them back after they'd done a good job. Soon the BSC business was booming, and when Dawn moved to Stoneybrook, they asked her to join. Everything went smoothly until Stacey had to move back to New York. By then, a year had gone by, the original club members were in the eighth grade, and Mal had joined them at SMS as a sixth-grader. She was old enough to sit (and she certainly had plenty of experience with young children), so they asked both Mal and me to replace Stacey. Then, of course, Stacey moved back here (I felt guilty that she couldn't move into her old house, since we were living in it), and she settled into the club routine again. We have seven members now, and Kristy says that's enough. I think she's right. Claud's bedroom is getting crowded.

How does the club run? Well, we meet three times a week, on Monday, Wednesday, and Friday afternoons from 5:30 until 6:00. People know that we meet then and they phone us to arrange sitters. They also know they must phone us at Claudia's, whose bedroom is BSC headquarters.

Kristy, as I mentioned, is our chairman. Her job is to conduct meetings, solve problems, get good ideas, and generally keep things running smoothly. These are two of Kristy's ideas: Kid-Kits, and the club notebook. Kid-Kits are terrific. Kristy suggested that we each get a cardboard box, decorate it, and fill it with things kids like to play with—our old books, games, and toys, plus stickers, colouring books, and art materials. We sometimes take the Kid-Kits with us when we babysit, and children *love* them. This is good for business, because when our charges are happy, then their parents are happy, and then the parents ask us to sit again.

The club notebook is a good idea, too, but not nearly as much fun. In it, each of us has to write up every single job we go on. I think that's a royal pain, but I have to admit it's helpful. Once a week we're supposed to read the notebook to see what happened while our friends were sitting, and often I find out how they solved difficult sitting situations, or learn about a problem a kid is having whom I'll be sitting for soon.

Claudia is the vice-chairman because we're always using (or eating) her things. Three times a week we take over her room. We use her phone and eat her junk food.

23

Claud's pretty good-natured about this. In fact, I think she likes having us around.

The job of the secretary, Mary Anne, is a big one. Mary Anne is in charge of the club *record* book (not the notebook), in which she keeps track of our clients, their addresses and phone numbers, and the rates they pay. More importantly, she schedules every single one of our sitting jobs. She has to keep track of all our other activities and appointments, such as my ballet lessons, Mal's orthodontist appointments, and Kristy's softball practices. I don't think Mary Anne has ever made a mistake.

Stacey is our treasurer. She's good with numbers. It's her job to keep a record of the money we earn (just for our interest), to collect subs from each of us every Monday, to preside over the treasury, and to dole out money when it's needed—to help Claudia pay for her phone bill, to replace items in the Kid-Kits that get used up, such as crayons, and to shell out for a club pizza party or pyjama party every now and then. The funny thing is, Stacey loves collecting money—*having* it—but hates parting with it, even though it isn't her own. Nothing pleases her more than the sight of a fat treasury envelope.

Dawn is our alternate officer. That means that if one of us has to miss a meeting, Dawn can take over that person's job. She's a bit like an understudy in a play. She has to know how to cope with the treasury, schedule appointments, etc.

Then there are Mal and me. As junior officers, we take on a lot of the afternoon sitting jobs. This is mostly because we aren't allowed to sit at night yet unless we're sitting for our own brothers and sisters. But it does mean that the other girls are free for evening jobs, so all in all we're important club members, too.

Believe it or not, there are a couple of other club members whom I haven't described yet. This is because they are associate members and don't come to meetings. They're our backups. They're responsible sitters we can rely on if a job comes up that none of us seven regular members can take, which does happen sometimes. Our associate members are Shannon Kilbourne, a friend of Kristy's, and . . . Logan Bruno, Mary Anne's boyfriend!

"Ahem," said Kristy loudly.

I looked up guiltily. I'd been daydreaming again. The rest of the BSC members had arrived and Kristy was starting the meeting. She called the meeting to order. Then Stacey collected our subs, gleefully exclaiming over the contents of the treasury and beaming when no one said they needed any money. After that, we waited for job calls to come in.

The first was from Mrs Rodowsky. She and her husband have three boys—Shea,

Jackie, and Archie. Jackie, the seven-year-old, is a walking disaster, completely accident-prone, but we love him.

I got the job.

When the phone didn't ring again for a while, we began talking.

"When's your aunt coming, Jessi?" Stacey wanted to know. (By then, practically the whole world knew my aunt was moving in.)

"I'm not sure," I said. "I mean, Aunt Cecelia isn't even sure. She still has to hire removal men, sell some of her furniture, things like that." I paused. Then, "Ohhh!" I moaned. "*Why* does she have to come? There must be some other solution to this problem. Perhaps my parents could hire a jailer."

Kristy giggled. But then she said, "Really, Jessi. How bad could having your aunt move in actually be? Nannie moved in with my family, and it's been great. We love having her around."

"And Mimi lived with us for as long as I can remember," added Claud. "You know how I felt about her. She was like another mother."

I knew. And I knew that Nannie was wonderful, too.

But Aunt Cecelia would *not* be wonderful, and my friends wouldn't understand that until they personally saw Aunt Cecelia in action.

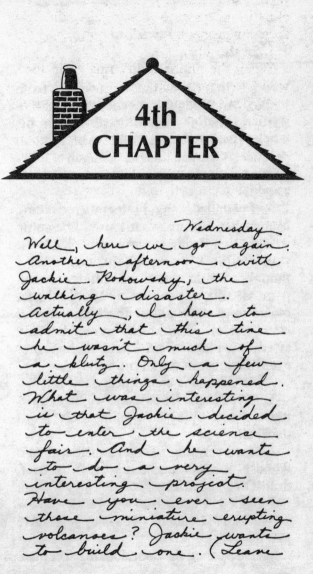

4th CHAPTER

Wednesday

Well, here we go again.
Another afternoon with
Jackie Rodowsky, the
walking disaster.
Actually, I have to
admit that this time
he wasn't much of
a klutz. Only a few
little things happened.
What was interesting
is that Jackie decided
to enter the science
fair. And he wants
to do a very
interesting project.
Have you ever seen
those miniature erupting
volcanoes? Jackie wants
to build one. (Leave

27

it to Jackie to choose the messiest possible project!) What have I got myself into?

I raced directly to the Rodowskys' from school. Mrs Rodowsky needed me by three-thirty so that she could drive Shea to his music lesson and little Archie to his football practice. (Can you imagine a bunch of four-year-olds playing football? It must be quite a sight.)

As I pedalled along, I remembered telling Mama that morning that I would be going straight to a sitting job after school. I knew she wouldn't worry about me. But, I thought, would things be different when Aunt Cecelia was in charge? Would she let me go to places without checking with her after school? Would she remember my afternoon plans when I told them to her over breakfast in the morning?

Aunt Cecelia is an old prune.

I arrived at the Rodowskys' right on time, parked my bike, and rang their front doorbell.

I heard running footsteps inside, then a whoosh, a crash, and a cry of, "Oh, drat, drat. Oh . . . *bull*frogs!"

I giggled. I knew that was Jackie.

"Jackie!" I called. "It's me, Jessi. Are you okay?"

Jackie opened the door, looking sheepish.

"I was running to answer the bell and I slipped on the rug and fell on my bottom."

I smiled, shaking my head. Then I let myself in and helped Jackie straighten out the rug.

"Jessi?" called Mrs Rodowsky. "Is that you?"

"Yes!" I replied. (I hoped she didn't think *I* had slipped on the rug.)

Mrs Rodowsky was in a rush.

"Archie!" she exclaimed. "You're supposed to be in your football kit. And, Shea, where are your piano books?"

The house was in turmoil for about five minutes—Jackie added to it by somehow getting his foot stuck in one of his old wellington boots—but finally Mrs R. and the boys were backing hurriedly down the drive. I was left with Jackie and the boot.

"I know I can get this off your foot," I told him.

"But what if you can't?" whimpered Jackie.

"Jackie," I said, "have you ever heard of someone who got a boot stuck on his foot and *never* got it off?"

"No," replied Jackie, as I braced myself against a wall and pulled.

"I wonder," said Jackie, trying not to slide forward. "You know, wellington boots are sometimes called galoshes. Is *one* boot called a galosh?"

"I haven't the faintest—*Oof*! Well, there

you are, Jackie. The boot's off. You're free."

"Thanks," he said gratefully.

Jackie wandered round the playroom, looking bored.

"What do you want to do?" I asked him.

"I don't know."

"Do you have any homework?"

"Nope. Well, not really. We're just supposed to think about whether we want to enter the science fair at school."

"Do you?" I asked him.

"*Me*? squeaked Jackie. "Are you kidding? I have such bad luck. I would never enter a contest. . . . Even though I think it would be fun to make a volcano."

"Fun to do *what*?" I repeated.

"Make a volcano. I saw it on *The Brady Bunch* once. You can build a model of a volcano, but it really works. I mean, lava really comes pouring out. That would be great. Lava everywhere."

The thought of "lava everywhere" made me feel a bit queasy. Even so, I said, "Jackie, you ought to make a volcano for the science fair! It would be a great project. Everyone else would probably just have, you know, things like leaf collections, or insects in jars, but *you* would build a *volcano* that would *erupt*. You'd win for sure."

Jackie looked doubtful. "I don't know," he said. "I bet some kids would do really, really good projects. I'm not very good at science. Besides, as I said, I have bad luck. I can't show a project to judges and an audience. Things never go right for me. Something bad would happen."

"Jackie. That's no way to talk. You've got to have confidence in yourself. A volcano—a spewing, dripping, running volcano—is a really terrific project. The kids would love it. More important, so would the teachers and judges."

"I don't know," said Jackie slowly.

"Oh, come on," I said. "This'll be great. Let's go to the library right now and see what kind of information we can find on volcanoes and how to make them. I'll leave a note for your mum in case she comes home early."

I didn't give Jackie a chance to say no. I just handed him his jacket, wrote the note, put on my own jacket, and marched Jackie to the public library. He barely said a word as we walked along.

When we reached the library, the first person we saw was Mrs Kishi, Claudia's mother! She's the head librarian.

"Hello," she greeted us, as we entered the children's section. "What are you two doing here?"

I explained Jackie's project to Mrs Kishi.

"Hmm," she said, "let's look in the science section."

Claud's mum helped us find three books. One was about volcanoes, one was about earth sciences, and the third was a book of science experiments, including a chapter called "How to Make an Erupting Volcano".

"Gosh," said Jackie. "I didn't think we'd find this. It's exactly what I need. It has all the instructions."

"You never know what you'll find in a library," said Mrs Kishi, smiling. Then she left Jackie and me sitting at a table with our books.

Jackie began to read about the exploding-volcano experiment. "You know," he said, "this doesn't look so easy. It says you have to make a frame out of wood and glass to put your volcano in. They didn't do that on *The Brady Bunch*."

"Well, *we're* going to," I informed him. "We're going to make the best project in your whole school."

"But there are words here I don't understand. The books says you have to get different coloured clay to make ig—iggy—"

"Igneous," I supplied.

"Okay. Igneous rocks. And . . . and metal—"

"Metamorphic rocks."

"And . . . oh, boy."

"Sedimentary rocks."

"Whoa," whispered Jackie. "And then you have to get stuff called, um—"

Even I had to pause for that one. "I'm not sure what this is," I said at last.

"So where are we going to get it?" asked Jackie worriedly.

"It says you can buy it at a chemist."

Jackie was quiet. He seemed stumped.

"What's wrong?" I asked him.

"On *The Brady Bunch* they just made a mound of papier-mâché or something and put this goo in and—*whoosh*! Why do I need to know about rocks? And why do I have to make a glass box? That sounds hard. And expensive. I've just spent all my pocket money."

"First of all," I replied, "as I said, we're going to make the best project in the school. I bet the volcano on *The Brady Bunch* didn't win a prize, did it?"

"No," answered Jackie triumphantly. "It was just for fun."

"Oh," I said. "Well, ours will be special. Also, I'm sure your parents will help you buy the materials for your project. Now, come on. Sit next to me. I have to learn all about volcanoes first. If you want to win at the science fair, you can't just make your volcano erupt. You have to tell the judges about volcanoes."

Jackie sat next to me while I learnt about lava and fire and fountains and ash and gas and some pretty disgusting things. He looked at the volcano experiment with a frown.

After about twenty minutes, I stood up.

"Well," I said, "I think I've got volcanoes sussed out now."

"Good," replied Jackie, "because I haven't."

"We'll take these books out and go home."

"Oh," said Jackie, brightening. "I haven't got my library tickets."

"Never mind. I've got mine," I told him.

So we took out the books and walked back to Jackie's house. When Mrs Rodowsky returned with Shea and Archie, she found Jackie and me still looking through the books. Well, Jackie was looking (sort of). I was making a list of materials he would need.

"Jackie's entering the science fair?" said Mrs Rodowsky, after I told her what we were doing. She looked both pleased and surprised.

"Yes," I said happily.

"But, Mum, we need clay and glass and some things from the chemist. It might be expensive," said Jackie.

"I don't think it'll be *too* expensive," said Mrs R. "Jackie, I'm so proud of you for wanting to work on a project. And, Jessi, thank you for inspiring him. I'm impressed that you convinced him to enter. Listen, would you mind helping Jackie with his project? The two of you seem to know what you're doing. Maybe you could arrange with the members of the Babysitters Club to be our only sitter between now and the science fair. That way you and Jackie will have plenty of time together."

"I think that's possible," I said. "I'll have to check with my friends, but I'm sure they'll understand."

"Great!" said Mrs R.

I left the Rodowskys' with a smile on my face. I knew I could help Jackie all the way to a prize.

5th CHAPTER

Saturday

Today, Dawn and I sat for my younger brothers and sisters. It was a fun afternoon, wasn't it?

Definitely, Mal. Your family is really something. With eight kids, you lot can come up with pretty good projects. I think the most ambitious thing Jeff and I ever did was set up a table in front of our house in California. We sold bunches of flowers that grew wild everywhere. Nobody bought any, of course. Oops, I'm off the subject.

That's okay. Well, to get back to our job, two things were going on. One, Margo *decided to enter the Stoneybrook Elementary science fair. Two, the other kids needed something to do so they... opened a true and actual lending library!*

It was a peaceful Saturday at Mal's house. Dawn had arrived to help her babysit, Mr and Mrs Pike had just left, all of Mal's brothers and sisters were at home, and nobody was arguing. Not even Nicky and the triplets. Dawn had brought over her Kid-Kit (Mallory's is no good at her own house, since it's mostly full of the Pikes' things), and Claire, Margo, and Vanessa were looking through it. The boys were playing their endless imaginary game about the Wandering Frog People. That has been going on for about two years now, which is one year and 364 days longer than Mal had hoped it would last. At any rate, the triplets were occupied.

"Look!" said Claire, peering eagerly into Dawn's Kid-Kit. "It's the new Sindy doll. Cool! She's got sleepover stuff with her."

"Here's a jigsaw puzzle," said Vanessa. "Ooh, this looks hard."

"It is," Dawn told her, "but I think you'll like it. When you put it together it's a poem. It's the one by Robert Frost about walking through woods on a snowy evening. And all around the poem are snowflakes."

"I'm going to try it," said Vanessa,

immediately dumping the pieces out on the floor. Vanessa loves to read and write poetry.

Margo looked half-heartedly through the box. She didn't seem to want to play with anything.

"Something wrong, Margo?" Mallory asked her. Margo has the world's weakest stomach. Mallory sincerely hoped it wasn't upset.

Margo shook her head. "I'm just thinking," she replied.

"About what?" asked Dawn.

"Well, our school is having a science fair and anyone can enter."

"Do you want to enter?" asked Mal. "I entered three times when I was at Stoneybrook Elementary. I'm not great at science, but the fair was a lot of fun anyway."

"It was?" said Margo. "Maybe I'll enter then. Our teacher said we'll get extra marks just for entering. Will you help me, Mallory?"

"Of course," replied Mal. "I mean, I'll *help* you, but I won't do your project *for* you. Deal?"

"Deal," said Margo. She grinned.

"Do you have any idea what you want to do your project on?" asked Dawn.

Margo thought for a while. "No," she said at last.

"Well, let's go upstairs and look at the books in our rooms," suggested Mallory. "We have some science books."

"Maybe we'll find the Wandering Frog People while we're at it," said Dawn, with a little smile.

Mallory looked up. The boys were gone. That wasn't much of a surprise, since Wandering Frog People is a very quiet game.

What was a surprise, though, was finding Nicky and the triplets in their room, poring over a set of encyclopaedias.

"What are you doing?" Mal asked her brothers as she and Margo stopped in the doorway.

"Looking up frog stuff," replied Jordan. "Adam says there's such a thing as an African tree toad, but I don't believe him."

"Don't we have a book on reptiles somewhere?" asked Mal.

"And I need to find a book about . . . about the sky," said Margo, suddenly inspired. "I want my project to be about constellations or maybe the planets."

"What we need is a library," said Mallory.

"Hey!" exclaimed Byron. "We could make a library right here in our rooms. Altogether, we have science books; mysteries; your horse stories, Mal; Claire's picture books; the Hardy Boys and Nancy Drew books" (Adam made a face at the mention of Nancy Drew); "Vanessa's poetry books; Nicky's dog stories; and all those other books." (The Pike kids get a lot of books on their birthdays and on holidays. They love reading.)

"Yeah . . ." said Nicky slowly. "A real library. Great."

"We could organize it like the public library," said Jordan, getting excited, too. "And we could really let kids around here borrow our books."

"We need a librarian," said Adam.

"Vanessa!" cried the others immediately. "Vanessa would be a great librarian. She's always reading or writing."

"But I have to work out my science-fair project," said Margo. "How can I do that while you're all having fun making a library?" Margo looked (and sounded) miffed.

"Easy," said the ever-practical Byron. "You help us with the library. Then, when it's all ready, you can go to the science section to work on your project. You can be our first customer."

"All *right*!" cried Margo.

"Margo, go and tell Dawn and Claire and Vanessa to come up here," said Jordan. "We'll need everyone to help us."

Margo turned and faced the stairs. "DAWN! CLAIRE! VANESSA!" she yelled. "COME HERE!"

"Margo," said Mallory, giggling, "Jordan could have done *that* himself."

It wasn't long before preparations for the library were underway. Mallory and Dawn were amazed at how organized the kids, especially the older ones, were about their project.

"First," said Byron, "we have to group the same kinds of books together. We've all got science books in our rooms. They should go on the same bookshelf. Margo, you've got your Secret Seven books; Vanessa, you've got Nancy Drews; and Nicky and I both have Hardy Boys. We should put those mystery series in another bookcase."

"I think all the animal stories should go together, too," said Nicky.

Well, for a while, the upstairs of the Pike house was a pretty big mess, with the kids carrying books back and forth, in and out of rooms.

"What are your parents going to say when they get home?" Dawn asked Mal, looking worried.

"Nothing! They'll love this!"

When the books had been organized, the kids divided themselves into four groups. Well, not exactly *groups*, since one of the groups consisted of just one person. Anyway, Vanessa, the chosen librarian, set up her desk as the checkout counter, and Claire helped her. Byron made signs that read ANIMAL STORIES, MYSTERIES, etc. Jordan and Margo made a huge stack of pockets to tape inside the covers of the books, and Adam and Nicky took index cards, wrote the title of one book on each card, and stuck it in the pocket that Jordan and Margo had just made. It was a real assembly line and took quite a bit of work, but by late that afternoon, the library was ready. The Pike kids looked satisfied.

Vanessa manned her desk. The others stood in the bedrooms, as library assistants, Mallory guessed. And Margo announced, "Here I am! Your first customer. I need to see the science section, please."

"Right over here," said Adam, pulling his sister into the boys' room. "What are you looking for?"

"I'm not sure," replied Margo. "I suppose books about space."

Adam handed Margo several books, she sat down at a desk, began reading, and . . .

"Now what?" asked Nicky. "Where are our other customers."

"Um, nobody else knows about your library," Dawn pointed out gently.

The Pike kids looked wounded, but just for a minute.

"We'll advertise!" said Vanessa.

"Yeah, we'll make a big sign that says 'Pike Library' and put it in the front garden!" exclaimed Jordan.

So the triplets made the sign, and then they, Nicky, and Claire went from house to house in the neighbourhood, telling all their friends about the *very* local public library. They returned with Matt and Haley Braddock.

"We're bored," said Haley, who's nine. "We need some new books to read."

Actually, Haley didn't just speak. She spoke and used sign language at the same time, since Matt, who's seven, is profoundly deaf and can't speak or hear.

"Yeah," signed Matt. "I want a book about baseball."

Beaming, Nicky helped the Braddocks find their books. While they were looking, the doorbell rang. Buddy and Suzi Barrett were on the front step, also wanting books.

"This is great!" cried Nicky. "Our library is working!"

Vanessa was busy at her desk. Whenever a customer found a book, she removed the card from the pocket, wrote on it the name of the person who was taking out the book, and also the day's date. Then she put the card aside and stuck a Post-It on the book pocket with the due date written on it.

"Overdue books cost you ten cents a day," she told each customer, "so bring them back on time."

Meanwhile, Margo had decided on her science project. "I am going to make a space house," she said. "It will show what life would be like if the moon was our home planet."

"Great!" said Mal.

When Mr and Mrs Pike returned, they were pleased with the Pike Library, but not pleased when Buddy Barrett returned his book during dinner that night. Byron had to add something to the sign in the front garden:

Open weekdays from 3:30 - 6:00 pm.
Open weekends from 10.00 a.m. - 5:00 pm.
Not open during meals!

6th
CHAPTER

Dum da-dum dum.

The dreaded day had arrived.

Aunt Cecelia was moving in.

It was the Saturday after the one when the Pike Library had opened. And it began early. Daddy and Mama were up at the crack of dawn. So was I. I was in the basement, practising at the *barre* Daddy had built for me, and scrutinizing my leg movements in the big mirror. But when I smelt coffee brewing in the kitchen, I went upstairs to see just how the awful day was going to start.

"She's hired a trailer," Daddy was telling Mama as I reached the kitchen. He was scrambling eggs while Mama cut up fruit.

"A trailer!" exclaimed Mama.

"Well, just a small one," said Daddy. "She's sold some of her things, put a lot of other things in storage, and the rest is moving here with her."

"Where's she going to put it all?" I asked.

"Good morning, Jessi," was Mama and Daddy's reply.

"'Morning," I answered. I didn't say *good* morning, because it wasn't.

"She's going to put it in the guest room. That will be her room. You know that," Mama told me.

"A whole trailer's worth of furniture?" I pressed.

Daddy gave me a look that plainly said, "Don't push it."

So I didn't.

At eight o'clock, Daddy left for Aunt Cecelia's. He would have to attach the trailer to our estate car and drive it back here while Aunt Cecelia drove her own car. I was pretty glad she had a car. That meant she wouldn't be stuck at our house day in and day out. As Kristy's big brother says, "A set of wheels is a necessity."

Daddy was gone a long time.

"He has to supervise the removal men," Mama explained to Becca and me as we ate lunch (our last meal without Aunt Cecelia). "And hooking the trailer to our car may take a little while."

Daddy and Aunt Cecelia arrived at our house at about two-thirty. Mama, Becca, Squirt, and I were sitting on the front step. We were sitting under a banner that read:

WELCOME, AUNT CECILIA. Mama had insisted that Becca and I make the banner, so we'd purposely spelt our aunt's name wrong. (Mama hadn't noticed.)

When the cars and the U-Haul pulled into our drive, Becca and I just looked at each other. We didn't even stand up until Mama nudged us and said, "What's happened to your manners?"

So we walked to the drive, trailing behind Mama.

Aunt Cecelia got out of her car, kissed us all, and then said, "Rebecca, don't slouch," and, "Jessica, *please* tidy up your hair."

What could we say? Becca stands like any normal eight-year-old, and I'd been practising all morning. Of course my hair was a mess.

"Well," said Daddy, sounding a little too cheerful, "let's all get Aunt Cecelia's things inside." We looked inside the trailer. It was *packed*!

I almost cried, "Where are we going to put all that stuff?" but I knew better. I just picked up a box and lugged it inside. Becca did the same.

After about half an hour, the guest room was overflowing, and there were still two chairs, this stupid bird cage on a stand (no bird in it), a little table, some lamps, a tea tray and even a small rug in the van. Not to mention more boxes.

"Mama," I said urgently, "those things

are *not* going to fit in Aunt Cecelia's room. You can barely walk around in there now."

"I know," Mama replied. "We'll find places for them."

"That's right." Aunt Cecelia had come up behind us. "A place for everything and everything in its place," she said primly.

I hadn't expected those places to be all over our house. We crammed a lot of things, including the bird cage, into the living room. The small rug was placed over a larger rug in the study. It looked terrible. One of the tables ended up in my room.

"Mama, *why* did she bring so much stuff?" Becca whispered when Aunt Cecelia was busy in the guest room. I mean, *her* room.

"Because it belongs to her. It's part of her past," Mama replied gently. "It reminds her of her life with her husband, and she misses your Uncle Steven very much."

For a moment, I felt sorry for Aunt Cecelia. But just for a moment. The next thing I knew, she was handing me two china eggs and asking me to put them in my room because there wasn't room in hers.

When she'd gone, I looked round my room. It was different. It didn't say "Jessi" any more. It said "Jessi and some old lady." Our house didn't feel like our house any more, either. Signs of Aunt Cecelia were everywhere.

Squirt was confused, and I didn't blame him one bit.

But Aunt Cecelia, looking at the not-yet-organized house said, "I'll have things in order in no time."

"I hope so," Mama replied. "I start my job on Monday."

Aunt Cecelia kept her word. By that evening, our house was tidy (but crowded), Aunt Cecelia had unpacked and put away all her stuff in her bedroom, and she'd folded the boxes, stacked them, and tied them up with string for the dustbin men to take away on Tuesday.

"She's efficient," Daddy remarked.

"She's a drill sergeant," I whispered to Becca.

"Girls, are you ready for bed?" Aunt Cecelia called upstairs.

Ready for bed? It was too early to go to bed. And why was Aunt Cecelia calling us, anyway?

"Not yet," I replied.

"Well, please put on your nightdresses."

Becca and I looked at each other, mystified. Then we put on our nightdresses, but we went downstairs afterwards to find out what Mama and Daddy were doing. Guess what? They were just sitting in the study, reading. Why weren't they stopping Aunt Cecelia?

"Mama," I whispered, "Aunt Cecelia

told me to get ready for bed, and it's only eight thirty."

"You don't have to go to bed yet," said Mama absently, but she was much more interested in her book than in the injustices Aunt Cecelia was carrying out against Becca and me.

My sister and I left the study.

"They weren't any help," said Becca.

"They're tired," I told her. "And Mama's probably enjoying this last weekend before she begins work. We should let them relax."

That was a bad move on our part.

The next morning, our family had just got up when Daddy said brightly, "I've got a great idea. Why don't we go out for brunch this morning? We'll celebrate your mother's new job and having my sister here with us."

"Oh, why don't you two go out alone?" Aunt Cecelia said to Daddy and Mama. "Now that I'm here, you can have a private brunch. Wouldn't that be nice? No children's menu to look at. No high chair to worry about. I'll stay here and babysit for Jessi and Becca and Squirt. After all, that's one reason I moved in."

Mama and Daddy were thrilled with the idea, but all I could think was, *She'll* stay here and babysit for *us*? On a Sunday morning? I could do that. I *have* done that.

But I kept my mouth shut.

So Mama and Daddy left, and Aunt Cecelia babysat for my sister and brother and me. And I *mean*, she babysat. She did everything for us. That's okay where Squirt's concerned, but Becca is too old to be reminded to use her serviette (she knows when to do that), and I'm *much* too old to be told to finish everything on my plate. Sometimes I can't. Besides, I have to watch my weight. I can't be a fat ballerina.

When our breakfast was finally over, I lifted Squirt out of his high chair and began to clean him up as I always do.

"I'll do that," said Aunt Cecelia. "You girls get dressed."

As Becca and I dragged ourselves upstairs, I said to my sister, "I've got a new name for Aunt Cecelia."

"What?" asked Becca.

"Aunt Dictator."

While Mama and Daddy were out, Aunt Cecelia left Squirt in his high chair (when *I* babysit, I play with him; it's much more stimulating for him) and prepared a salad for lunch, and also began preparing dinner. Aunt Cecelia was so busy cooking that she hadn't got round to cleaning up Squirt yet.

"Aunt Di—I mean, Aunt Cecelia," I said, entering the kitchen, "Becca and I are going to take Squirt for a walk." (After I wash his face and hands, I thought.)

I was dressed. And my hair was tidy.

Aunt Cecelia wouldn't be able to find anything to complain about.

"Where are you going to take him?" she asked.

"Just up and down the street like we usually do." I paused, then added, "I put him in his buggy and strap him in, and I never let him lean over and touch the wheels because he might get hurt."

Aunt Dictator looked outside. "Too cloudy," she announced.

I nearly exploded, but instead I said, "Okay. Then I'm going over to Mallory Pike's house."

"Who's Mallory?" my aunt asked.

"You met her once," I told her. "She's my best friend."

"Where does she live?"

"Nearby. I can ride my bike to her house."

"I don't think so." Aunt Dictator shook her head slowly. "No, I don't think so. I'm in charge now, and it looks like rain. The roads will get too slippery for bicycles."

That did it. I turned round and stomped out of the kitchen.

"Walk like a lady!" Aunt Cecelia called after me.

I didn't answer her. (But I did stop stomping.) Who did Aunt Cecelia think she was? Oh, yeah. My babysitter.

I ran upstairs to Becca's room. My poor sister had followed me to the kitchen before, but when she saw how unreasonable Aunt Cecelia was being, she had escaped back to her room. Becca is a little shy and very sensitive to criticism, so she wasn't about to face Aunt Cecelia until she thought the arguing was over.

"Becca," I said, "you can stop hiding now. I've got an idea. It's time to start our Aunt Cecelia project."

I whispered into Becca's ear, and she began to giggle. By the time Mama and Daddy returned, my sister and I had been hard at work. We'd turned Aunt Dictator's bed into an apple-pie bed. We'd filled one of her slippers with Daddy's shaving cream. We'd put a realistic rubber spider on her pillow and covered it with the bedspread.

Her room looked normal, but we knew better. Mama and Daddy couldn't see what we'd done, but when Aunt Dictator put on her slippers or got into bed, what would happen?

Would Mama and Daddy see how unfair our new sitter was? Would they give Aunt Cecelia a talking-to? Or would Becca and I just be in an awful lot of trouble?

Surprisingly, none of the above happened. At eleven o'clock that night, Aunt Cecelia was reading in bed. Mama stuck her head into the room to thank her for making her life so much easier. And all Aunt Cecelia said was, "You're welcome," even though she must have found the shaving cream and the spider. And she must have had to make her bed up again.

I didn't know what to think of that.

7th CHAPTER

"Goodbye, Mama! Good luck!" I called.

"Have fun at work!" Becca added.

It was the next morning, and Mama and Daddy were leaving for their jobs together. I felt as though I was sending Mama off to her first day at nursery school.

My parents' cars rolled down the drive. It was time for Becca and me to get a move on or we'd be late for school.

"Take care of Squirt," Becca said seriously to Aunt Dictator, strapping her rucksack on and picking up her lunch box.

"Yeah," I said. "Remember, he's allowed to watch *Sesame Street*, and he always needs an afternoon nap and usually a morning nap, too. And he likes to take a bottle of water to bed with him. Oh, and—"

Suddenly I stopped talking. Whoa. If looks could kill.

54

"Jessica," said my aunt crisply. "I've raised children of my own."

You didn't raise Squirt, I thought.

I was not in a good mood by the time I left for school.

But when I came home that afternoon, I was in a much better frame of mind. I'd got an A in a maths test, I'd scored three goals during netball, my English teacher had said he was impressed with the story I was working on, and I had a full (and Aunt Cecelia-free) afternoon ahead of me. I was supposed to babysit at the Rodowskys' and then go to the Monday BSC meeting.

I bounced through our front door. "Hello!" I called.

"SHHH!" was Aunt Cecelia's reply. "Your brother's asleep."

"*Now*?" I said. "He's usually awake by this time."

"Well, he isn't today."

Auntie Dictator, Auntie Dictator, Auntie Dictator, I sang to myself.

I put away my rucksack hastily, changed my clothes, and dashed into the kitchen for a quick snack. I had to be at the Rodowskys' soon.

Aunt Cecelia was standing at the cooker when I came in. I opened the fridge and surveyed the snack possibilities.

"Snack's on the table," said Aunt Cecelia, without turning round to look at me. (I think some adults actually *do* have eyes

55

behind their heads. The eyes are just hidden by their hair, that's all.)

I looked at the table.

Milk and biscuits. Kids' stuff.

"I usually have a sandwich," I said, opening the fridge again.

"Not this close to dinner, you don't. You'll spoil your appetite."

"But I *do* get to eat a sandwich. Mama lets me. We eat lunch really early. Before it's even twelve o'clock."

"Two biscuits," said Aunt Cecelia.

"I'll pass," I told her. "I'll eat at Jackie's house."

"Jackie? Who's Jackie? Not a boy, I hope."

"As a matter of fact, Jackie *is* a boy."

"Well, you're certainly not spending the afternoon with a *boy*."

"Aunt Cecelia, he's seven years old. I babysit for him."

My aunt was about to protest when Becca came home, as starving as I was. She also requested a sandwich and got two measly biscuits instead. Since she ate hers, I ate mine after all. (Oh, I think I forgot to mention that the biscuits weren't anything yummy, like chocolate chip. They were oat-bran bars.)

"Okay," I said, jumping up from the table. "Gotta go! I'll be at the Rodowskys' until just after five. Then I'll be at Claudia Kishi's for our Babysitters Club meeting."

"Wait a minute," said Aunt Cecelia. "Where are you going?"

"To the Rodowskys' and then to Claudia's."

"I don't know those people."

"But I do."

"But I can't let you go running off to strange places."

"They *aren't strange*!"

"They are to me."

"Aunt Cecelia, you don't understand. This sitting job is my responsibility. I babysit all the time. You have to let me go."

"I don't *have* to let you do anything," said Aunt Dictator. "Besides, *you* are *my* responsibility now. I'm in charge while your parents are out. If anything happens to you, I'm—"

"I know. You're responsible," I said. "But I have a commitment. I told the Rodowskys a week ago that I would babysit this afternoon. They're counting on me. And a good babysitter never lets her clients down. Unless there's an emergency," I added.

Aunt Cecelia looked thoughtful.

"You can call Mama or Daddy at work and tell them what my plans are. They'll say I can go. This is my schedule. And these are *my* responsibilities."

"All right," said Aunt Cecelia at last. "What time will you be home?"

"Ten past six. Babysitters Club meetings

always end at six o'clock. Then I cycle home."

Aunt Cecelia nodded. "Very well, then."

I made a dash for the door—for two reasons. 1. I was about to be late. 2. I didn't want Aunt Dictator to change her mind.

I had to *speed* to the Rodowskys'. I was glad Aunt Cecelia couldn't see me. I didn't break any laws, but I nearly broke my head riding over a curb. I arrived at Jackie's house in one piece, though.

"Hi," I greeted Mrs Rodowsky, breathlessly. I glanced at my watch. "Boy, I've just made it. I'm sorry I was almost late." (A good babysitter tries to get to any job, even the most routine one, a few minutes early in case the parents have special instructions, or there's a problem, such as a child who's going to cry a lot when Mummy leaves.)

"Don't worry, Jessi," said Mrs R. as she let me inside. "I know I can count on you."

I wish Aunt Cecelia would count on me, I thought.

A few minutes later, Mrs R. left with Shea. Archie was supposed to have gone with her—to be dropped off at football practice—but he had stayed at home that day, recovering from an ear infection.

"He's on the mend, though," his mother had told me. "He'll be back at school tomorrow. He doesn't need to stay in bed, and don't worry about medicine. I'll give him his next dose at suppertime."

So I was left with Jackie and Archie.

"Okay," I said enthusiastically to Jackie. "Let's get to work on your volcano. Did your mum and dad buy the things you need?"

"Yup," replied Jackie.

He and Archie and I were in the Rodowskys' playroom. Archie looked at his big brother and me with interest. "Can I help?" he asked.

"This is Jackie's project," I told Archie.

"Oh. Can I watch, then?"

"Of course," I replied. I turned to Jackie. "Now the first thing we need to do is build that box, the glass one with the wooden frame that we'll put our volcano in," I said.

"*Our* volcano?" asked Jackie.

"I mean yours. Now let's see. Where are the instructions?"

"You don't have to worry about that," said Jackie. "My dad and I made a box over the weekend. It doesn't look exactly like the one in the picture, but it's glass, and it's big enough for the volcano."

"Oh, good," I said. I felt relieved. Building the box had sounded difficult, even harder than making a working volcano. "Then we can get started on the next step," I told Jackie.

"Yea! Papier-mâché!" he cried. (Just the *idea* of something messy appeals to Jackie.)

"Nope," I said, referring to the instructions. "First we have to build up the layers

59

of igneous, metamorphic, and sedimentary rock. We'll use the Plasticine for that. Did you buy three different colours of Plasticine?"

"What's Plasticine?" asked Archie, who was beginning to look bored.

"Modelling clay," I told him. "Did you get some, Jackie?"

"Yup. We got red, yellow, and brown. But, Jessi, *clay* doesn't look like rocks." Jackie sounded worried.

"It doesn't matter," I told him. "It's supposed to *represent* rocks."

"Can't we just build a volcano?" he asked.

"Not if you want to win a prize in the fair. You have to do a really terrific project. Now where's the clay? And the box?"

Jackie laid out the materials on an old table in the playroom. He watched while I built up the layers of rock that lie under volcanoes. It didn't take me too long.

"Goody!" he exclaimed as soon as I'd finished. "Papier-mâché time!"

Before I knew it, Jackie was mixing flour and water, and Archie was tearing strips of newspaper. Apparently, they had made papier-mâché before.

"Goop, goop, goop," sang Jackie, as he slurped his hands in and out of the pasty bowl. "Hey, this is a good batch, Archie," he said. Jackie was up to his elbows in goo. He grinned happily.

"Okay," I instructed, "take the papier-mâché and build a mountain on top of the clay, and around this tin can. Don't fill the can in. That's where we'll put the chemicals to make the lava."

"Mmmm," said Jackie. He held up his hands and let the goop drip back into the bowl. Then he got an itch and wiped his cheek, leaving papier-mâché smeared across it.

I tried to ignore that. I read up on igneous, metamorphic, and sedimentary rocks. But in the background, I was aware of cries of, "Got you! I'm the slime monster!" and, "Hey, Archie, look. If you wrap the papier-mâché around your arm you can make a cast," and, "Cool. Wrap me *all* up, Jackie. Make me a mummy!"

I glanced at the boys. They were having the time of their lives. Papier-mâché was everywhere—except surrounding the can in the glass box. Jackie hadn't started his mountain yet.

"This is good fun!" he exclaimed, just as I was about to tell him to get to work. "I can't wait to see lava, lava everywhere!"

I looked at my watch. "Time to clear up, you two," I said. "Your mum and Shea will be home soon."

"You know what, Jessi?" Jackie replied. "This was the best afternoon of my life!"

8th CHAPTER

Thursday

Another afternoon with David Michael and Emily Michelle. Nanny was practising with her bowling team. I'm glad she gets out in the afternoons, because her mornings are spent entirely with Emily. Anyway, it was a pretty quiet afternoon, but even so, something intresting happened:

Jackie and Margo now have one more competitor in the science fair. I'd never have guessed it, but David Michael wants to enter, so I tried to help him choose a project and work with Emily on naming the parts of her body at the same time. It was a challenging and fun afternoon. I'm still thinking of becoming a teacher some day.

Uh-oh. I should have known.

Competition.

When Kristy gets involved in something, the competition heats up right away. (I bet if you opened a dictionary and looked up "competition", you'd find a picture of Kristy's face.)

Kristy now saw the science fair as a competition between Mallory, herself, and me, as well as between all the kids at the fair. It would be as if . . . well, if David Michael won, Kristy would have won. In other words, she would have beaten me. At least that's what I thought at first. Things turned out quite differently.

Anyway, Kristy was babysitting that afternoon. Nannie had just driven off in her car, the Pink Clinker, and Kristy was trying to think of something fun to do with her little brother and sister. Usually, David Michael wants to play outside, but that afternoon he curled himself up in an armchair with his second-grade science book and began poring over it.

"What are you doing?" asked Kristy. (David Michael practically has to be bolted to his desk to do the small amount of homework he sometimes gets. He's bright but he doesn't like school much, and he *really* doesn't like homework, particularly during the softball season.)

"Well," said David Michael, "there's

going to be this science fair at school. Do you know what that is?"

Kristy hid a smile. Of course she knew what it was. She'd gone to Stoneybrook Elementary herself and had entered several of the fairs. But all she said was, "Yes."

"So *I* might enter it," said David Michael casually.

"Oh, yeah?" Kristy replied, just as casually.

"Yeah. There are prizes."

David Michael continued to flip through the book, while Kristy kept an eye on Emily, who was stacking blocks nearby.

"But," David Michael went on, "I'm not too good at science."

"You could enter anyway," Kristy told him. "Science isn't my best subject, either, but it's fun to enter the fair. Is there anything about science that you like?"

"Space," said David Michael immediately. "Aliens. Flying saucers."

"Some people say that's science *fiction*," Kristy told him. "You know. Made-up science."

"Well, I still like to think about Mars and Pluto and all the planets. I like Saturn best, because of its rings."

"Well, do a project on the solar system," said Kristy.

"Make a list of all our planets?" suggested David Michael.

"No. Something a little more ambitious.

Go out there and show what you can *really* do. Like when you're up to bat in a softball game. Think, 'I can do something big'."

"I'll make a huge Saturn!" cried David Michael, inspired. "I'll use a beach ball, and I'll put hoops round it for rings.'"

"That's the spirit," said Kristy, "but it isn't science-y enough. You're going to be competing against some kids who are playing hardball."

"Huh?"

"Kids who really know about science. Kids who will do great experiments. You've got to do something better than them if you want to win."

"Help me, Kristy," said her brother, plaintively.

Kristy paused. "I'll *help* you," she said at last, "but I won't do the project for you. Just like I can give you pointers on how to pitch a ball, but when you're on the pitcher's mound during a game, *you've* got to throw the ball, not me. Okay?"

"Okay." David Michael turned back to his desk.

"Hey, Emily," Kristy said, "what are you building?"

Emily looked up from a messy tower she was working on. "Building," she repeated, smiling.

"You're building a building?"

Emily looked frustrated. "No!"

"*What* are you building?" Kristy repeated patiently.

"Bwocks."

Kristy sighed. Emily Michelle is what the paediatrician calls "language delayed". And it's no wonder. The first part of her short life was spent in an orphanage in Vietnam, where she was spoken to in a foreign language (Vietamese, of course), when she was spoken to at all. Then she was uprooted at the age of two and flown to a completely new country where she didn't understand a word anyone said to her. Believe it or not, *Claudia* has been working with Emily some afternoons, teaching her vocabulary and concepts and other things that most two-year-olds already know.

Emily looked frustrated with her block-building, so Kristy decided to give her something new to do.

"Hey, Emily," she said. She led her away from the blocks. "Show me your *nose*. Where is your *nose*?"

"Nose," said Emily, pointing to it proudly.

"Good girl!" cried Kristy. (Claudia said that Emily learned fastest when she was praised for her good work.)

Then, without being asked, Emily pointed to her eye, and said triumphantly, "Eye!"

"Great!" exclaimed Kristy. "Where's your ear?"

Emily pointed. "Ear."

"Oh! I've just thought of a great song for you, Miss Emily," said Kristy suddenly. "Come over here. We need space."

Kristy led Emily to the middle of the study away from furniture. "Watch this," she said, and sang a song she'd learned at nursery school.

Head, shoulders, knees and toes, knees and toes.
Head, shoulders, knees and toes, knees and toes.
Eyes and ears and nose and mouth and chin.
Head, shoulders, knees and toes!

Kristy pointed to each body part as she sang the word. The song is fun, especially when you get going fast. (I can't wait until Squirt's old enough for it.)

Emily had smiled while she watched Kristy. Now Kristy took her sister's hands and placed them on her head and shoulders and so forth as she sang the song again. Emily laughed.

Kristy and Emily were going through the song for the fourth time when David Michael cried, "I've got it!"

"What?" asked Kristy.

"I'll draw a picture of each planet in our solar system. I'll colour them in really carefully and I'll write their names by them."

"We-ell," said Kristy. "Are you putting your heart into this?"

"Suppose not," replied David Michael. "Hey! How about if I get all my space monsters and all my astronauts and show them having a big, big, fight . . . on Venus?"

Kristy hesitated.

"I know, I know. Not good enough," said David Michael.

An hour went by. David Michael suggested several more ideas to Kristy, who kept encouraging him to go one step further. Kristy and Emily sang their new song together.

It was just before Kristy's mum and Watson came home from work that David Michael jumped up from his chair and announced, "This time I really *do* have a great idea!"

"What?" asked Kristy, who was losing hope.

"I'll build a mobile and it will show all the planets. I mean, I'll hang them in the right order: Mercury, Venus, Earth, Mars. You know. And I'll put the sun in the centre. Maybe I'll even make moons. At least, I'll make *our* moon."

"Now *that*," said Kristy, "sounds like a good idea. You'd really be showing something. Maybe you could even fix up the mobile so the planets could turn around each other."

"Maybe . . ." said David Michael uncertainly. But Kristy said he was pretty excited when his mum and Watson came home. He told them all about the science fair and his solar system mobile.

Then Emily had to show off, too. "Eyes and ears and nose and mouf and shin," she sang happily. Kristy couldn't get her to sing the rest of the song, but it didn't matter. David Michael was already clamouring for Kristy's help with his project.

Kristy and David Michael were now official competition in the science fair.

9th CHAPTER

Friday

I've always heard of playing music to plants, but I've never seen it done — until today. I was babysitting for Charlotte Johanssen, and she was working on her project for the Stoneybrook Elementary science fair. Okay, you lot, I know that some of you are helping kids get ready for the fair. Well, now I am, too. And I don't want to brag or anything, but you know how bright Charlotte is. She's a year ahead of herself in school. Anyway, I gave her a couple of suggestions for her experiment (she is conducting an actual experiment) and she caught on right away. Her work was interrupted when Becca Ramsey came over, though. Poor Becca. I feel sorry for her. You too, Jessi.

When Stacey arrived at the Johanssens' on Friday afternoon, Charlotte didn't run for the door as she usually does when she knows Stacey's going to be her sitter. Instead, Dr Johanssen answered the bell.

"Hi, Stacey," she said. "How are you feeling?" (Dr Johanssen knows about Stacey's diabetes and has been a help sometimes, even though she isn't Stacey's doctor.)

"Still a bit funny these days," Stacey admitted. "I'll probably see my doctor in New York soon."

"Well, that's good. Remember, you can always call me if you or your mum have any questions."

"Thanks," replied Stacey gratefully.

Dr Johanssen led Stacey into the kitchen. "Charlotte's as busy as a bee in here," she said. "I'll let Char tell you what she's doing, but I've got to get to the clinic now. You know where the emergency numbers are. Mr Johanssen will be home early today—around five o'clock or five-fifteen. You'll have plenty of time to get to your club meeting this afternoon."

"Okay," said Stacey. "Thanks. See you!"

"See you," Charlotte echoed absently, not looking up from her work.

Dr Johanssen smiled, shook her head, and left.

"What are you doing, Char?" asked Stacey. "What's your project?"

"It's not a project. It's an experiment."

Charlotte is only eight years old, but she's very bright. She's an excellent reader and does extremely well in school.

"An actual experiment?" said Stacey. "You mean you're going to discover something?"

"I hope so."

"Tell me what you're doing."

"Okay," said Charlotte eagerly.

In front of her were three jam jars. They had been cleaned thoroughly. In the bottom of each jar was some damp, white stuff.

"Well," said Charlotte, "my experiment will show if music helps plants grow better, or if some *kinds* of music help plants grow better."

"What's that white stuff?" asked Stacey, pointing to the bottoms of the jars.

"Wet cotton wool balls," Charlotte told her. "Can you believe it? If you bury seeds in damp cotton wool, they'll start growing faster than if you put them in ordinary soil. So I put three broad bean seeds in each jar. The seeds are just beginning to sprout. I keep the jars on this windowsill here in the kitchen. They all get sunlight part of the day. And I water them the same amount each day. *But*, here's the difference. Every afternoon, I take this jar, Jar Number One, upstairs to my room and play classical music to it for half an hour. I close the door so the other plants can't hear the music. Then, I bring Jar Number One downstairs, and take Jar Number Two upstairs. I play rock-and-roll music to those beans. I play it at exactly the same volume as I played the classical music."

"What about Jar Number Three?" asked Stacey, already impressed with what Charlotte was doing.

"Oh, I don't play any music to that one. Because maybe music *isn't* good for plants. After all, plants that grow wild don't hear music."

"And I suppose you're keeping track of how the plants grow and things like that," said Stacey.

"What?"

"Well, you're charting them or something, aren't you?"

"No. I mean, look at them. You can see for yourself. The sprouts in Jar Number One are bigger than in the other two jars. Those are the sprouts that hear classical music. I bet they're going to be tallest."

"But what if they were tallest, but the plants that heard the rock-and-roll music grew thicker than the others? Or their leaves were brighter or something?"

Stacey was going to keep on talking, but Charlotte got the message straight away. "Oh, wow!" she exclaimed. "I've got to keep all kinds of records and things, haven't I? I should make charts and graphs. I should measure the plants every day." She giggled. "I could keep a growth chart for them just like Mummy and Daddy kept for me when I was little. And I could make a chart showing their colouring and—and what else did you say, Stacey?"

"The thickness of the plants."

"Oh, yeah. Boy, I've got a lot of work to do."

Charlotte assembled crayons, a pencil, a ruler, graph paper, and plain white paper on the kitchen table. Stacey sat down next to her to watch her work. But before Charlotte began, she jumped up, exclaiming, "Oops! I forgot! I've got to take Jar Number One upstairs. It needs its music."

Charlotte carried the jar up the stairs, and soon Stacey could hear a few strains of what she thought was some music by Vivaldi. (Mrs McGill loves Vivaldi.) Then Charlotte must have closed her door, because the music dissolved into silence.

For a while after that, Stacey and Charlotte sat at the kitchen table. Char worked hard, occasionally asking Stacey for suggestions for help. Then, after a while, Charlotte glanced up, looking like the timid child she used to be.

"Stacey?"

"Yeah, Char?"

"Do you think that maybe—I mean, if you have time—you could come to the science fair? Only if you want to. It's just a kids' thing. I know that. And you're thirteen, but—"

"Charlotte, you know I'll be there. If you want me there, I'll come. Even if you hadn't invited me, I probably would have come, anyway. You're like my sister. I'm interested in everything you do."

"Thank you, Stacey!" exclaimed Charlotte, jumping up to give her a hug.

Charlotte settled down to work again, and Stacey admitted to me later that she couldn't help thinking that Char's project for the science fair was the best one she'd heard of so far. It was a real experiment. Although if Jackie's volcano really did erupt, that *would* be pretty exciting.

A few moments later, the doorbell rang.

"Do you want me to get it?" asked Stacey.

"Please," said Charlotte. "Half an hour's up, and I've got to swap jars and music now."

So Stacey answered the door. Guess who was standing on the front step? Becca—my own sister and Charlotte's best friend.

"Come on in," said Stacey.

Becca stepped inside, looking glum.

"What's wrong?" Stacey asked.

"Everything," mumbled Becca. "Where's Charlotte?"

"Upstairs. She'll be right down, though. She's working on her project for the science fair."

"Oh, yeah. The plants."

Charlotte trotted downstairs then. "Hi," she said. "Well, Jar Number Two is listening to Duran Duran." She paused. "Becca? What's the matter?"

"Oh, it's Aunt Dictator," said Becca, flopping into a chair in the living room.

Char and Stacey couldn't help giggling. "*Aunt Dictator?*"

"Yeah. That's what Jessi calls Aunt Cecelia."

"What's your aunt doing?" asked Charlotte.

"What *isn't* she doing!" Becca countered. "You know, Aunt Cecelia is supposed to be a babysitter, but she could do with some lessons. She isn't like you lot at all," she said to Stacey. (Stacey guessed that "you lot" meant the members of the BSC.) "She never listens to Jessi and me; she just orders us around. And she doesn't believe us. She doesn't trust us, either. It was like when I got stranded on the island with Dawn and everyone the weekend Mama and Daddy left Jessi in charge. When Jessi called Aunt Cecelia to tell her about the emergency, Aunt Cecelia raced to Stoneybrook and took charge as if Jessi didn't even exist.

"And," Becca went on, "she *thinks* she's so great with Squirt, but she isn't. She leaves him in his playpen when he should be walking around exploring things, or playing with me.

"You know what else is weird? Jessi and I have been playing all these practical jokes on Aunt Dictator, and she hasn't said a *word* about them."

"What kinds of jokes?" Charlotte wanted to know.

Becca explained, and Charlotte giggled helplessly.

"We think," said Becca, "that if we do enough awful things, Aunt Cecelia will get fed up and leave."

Stacey let the girls go ahead and plot Aunt Cecelia's demise. She didn't think Becca would carry out any of their ideas, and maybe taking imaginary action would make Becca feel better.

The girls discussed: tying Aunt Cecelia to a chair and telling the Ramseys that robbers had done it; hiding Aunt Cecelia's hair combs, so that she couldn't look perfect one morning; dressing up as Avon ladies and selling Aunt Cecelia jars full of water; colouring Squirt's beautiful curls with wash-out green dye; and other things bound to drive poor Aunt Cecelia up the wall.

Stacey laughed along with the girls, but she was worried. There are serious problems in the Ramsey household, she thought.

10th
CHAPTER

"I wonder what the world record for a paper chain is," said Mal thoughtfully as she and I worked dutifully at ours.

"I don't know," I replied. "Maybe we could look it up in the *Guinness Book of Records* under 'Paper Chain, Longest'."

It was Wednesday afternoon. Mal and I were in Claudia's room, waiting for a BSC meeting to begin.

"Claud?" I asked. "Do you have the *Guinness Book of Records* here?"

"Yes, but I don't know where it is," she replied. She was separating the contents of a packet of Lovehearts, pushing all the violet-coloured ones aside. Claud doesn't like purple Lovehearts.

"Oh," said Mal. "Well, I'll look it up at home. You know, if by some chance our paper chain beats the record, then I think we should try to weave the world's longest friendship bracelet next."

"But what would be the point?" I asked. "No one could wear it."

"So what? No one can eat a five hundred-pound pancake, but people are always making things like that, trying to set records."

"I know," I replied, "but five hundred people could each eat a *piece* of the pancake," I pointed out.

"Would you want to eat something that four hundred and ninety-nine other people were touching? And that had probably been buttered by an army of people skating across it with slabs of butter strapped to the bottoms of their shoes?"

"You two! Stop it!" exclaimed Mary Anne, looking absolutely green as she entered club headquarters and heard that last comment.

"Yeah, Mal. What's got into you?" I asked. "You'd think Aunt Dictator lived at *your* house."

"Nothing. I'm just pointing out to you lot that—"

"Order! Order! It's now five-thirty," Kristy interrupted.

I looked round. All seven of us were assembled in our usual places. Since it was a Wednesday, Stacey didn't have to collect subs.

"Any club business?" asked Kristy, as she always does.

"Logan babysat for the Arnold twins and Marilyn accidentally locked herself in the basement," said Mary Anne. "Logan had to rescue her through the outside cellar door."

We giggled.

"I know it sounds funny," Mary Anne continued, "but we should remember how that basement door works."

"Right," agreed Kristy. "Everybody, make a mental note of that."

(Claudia pretended to write something across her forehead.)

The phone rang then and Dawn answered it. "Hi, Mrs Perkins. . . . A week from Saturday? I'll ask Mary Anne to check, and I'll phone you straight back."

Dawn hung up the phone. "The Perkinses have a big party to go to. They need someone to babysit a week from Saturday," she told Mary Anne. "It'll be a late night."

Mary Anne was already looking through the record book. "Hmmm," she said. "Believe it or not, we're all busy. We'll have to phone Logan or Shannon. I'll take care of it."

In the end, Kristy's friend Shannon ended up with the job for the Perkinses. Then the BSC members waited for the phone to ring again. It didn't. So we began talking.

"You lot should see Margo's entry for the science fair," said Mal. "I want her to win, and I'm helping her when she asks for help, but mostly she's working on her own. I don't know what kind of research she's doing, but she seems to have decided that Barbie, Ken, and Skipper inhabit the moon, and that they dress in pink and silver sparkly outfits, a bit like the ones that the Jetsons used to wear. You know, on that old cartoon show?"

"Yes," said several of us, laughing.

"So then I asked Margo what people on the moon would eat, and she said, "Well, I suppose they couldn't grow any food in moon dust. They'd have to bring food with them like the astronauts did. So she put little plastic pastries and eggs and things from her doll's house into the space ship. To be honest," Mal finished up, "the space ship looks like a Barbie scene with a picture of the earth in the background."

"Why don't you correct her?" I asked. "Help her start again. Give her some books to read. Make her do it right."

"Nope. That's not what I'm there for," said Mal. "As her sister *or* her babysitter. This is her project. She's got to learn for herself."

"Well, she won't win," spoke up Kristy. She paused. "But then, David Michael isn't going to win, either. He's making a model of the planets in the solar system, remember? I told you all about that."

We nodded.

"He happened to choose a very tough

project. It's difficult to set up the planets so that they're at different distances from the sun. Right now, he's got them all going around the sun in one big circle—Mercury followed by Venus followed by Earth, and so on. I tried to show him a way to get the distance right, but he doesn't understand what I mean and he won't let me do it for him. I don't blame him. I'm the most competitive person here—I think—" (Claudia snorted), "but I'm not going to do his project for him. That's his job and we both know it. This is like the Little Miss Stoneybrook Pageant, in a way." (The pageant Kristy was referring to had been held in Stoneybrook a while back. A whole load of the kids we sit for wanted to enter. We could train them and coach them and rehearse them all we wanted, but when it got down to the big day, the kids were on their own.) "David Michael has to work his project out himself."

"How come?" I asked. "We rehearsed the girls for the pageant."

"That was different," said Mal. "We *rehearsed* them, but we couldn't get up on stage for them."

That was when I began to see that my friends and I weren't going to be as competitive as I'd first thought.

"Stacey," I said, after we'd taken a couple of job calls, "aren't you giving Charlotte a lot of help with *her* project?"

"Not really. I suggested that she needed some—what do you call it?—some data, to show the results of her experiment. I didn't say much more than that and Charlotte was off and running, making graphs, keeping charts."

Hmm, I thought.

"How's Jackie's volcano coming along?" Dawn asked me.

"Terrific!" I said. "I hate to say this, but I think Jackie's project is going to be the best one at the fair." (I couldn't help bragging.) "I think it'll win first prize. His volcano isn't just going to explode, it's going to show the structure of a volcano. You know, the kinds of rocks a volcano sits on, all that stuff."

"And Jackie did this research by himself?" asked Mal incredulously.

"Well, no. I found the books for him. And I told him about igneous, metamorphic, and sedimentary rocks. And I'm helping him build the volcano around a tin can."

There was a silence in club headquarters.

Finally, Mary Anne said, "Jessi, it sounds like you're doing Jackie's project *for* him. . . Not being rude or anything."

"No, I'm not!" I exclaimed. "I'm not doing it for him. He's right there when I read about volcanoes or when I work on his project. He knows what's going on." I stopped talking. I listened to what I'd just said. *Was* I doing Jackie's project for him? Nah. I just wanted to give him a lot of help so he could win for once in his life.

"You're sure you're not taking over?" asked Mal. "Maybe by accident?"

"No way! Of course not. But I'll tell you who *is* taking over. Aunt Cecelia. She won't let Becca or me do *any*thing on our own. It's rules, rules, rules. She lays out our clothes for us each night. She practically cuts our meat up for us. Becca and I know she doesn't trust us. I mean, not like she thinks we'd steal or anything. It's just that she doesn't believe we're capable of doing things that an eleven-year-old and an eight-year-old *are* capable of.

"If Aunt Cecelia were a good babysitter, she'd trust us. Our *parents* trust us. I mean, they set limits, but they do trust us. They let me use the oven and cook. They let us choose our own clothes. Not necessarily in shops, but once we have the clothes they let us decide what to wear to school or to a restaurant or wherever we're going. Aunt Cecelia doesn't trust us to do *any*thing right."

"Jessi, have you and Becca spoken to your parents about Aunt Cecelia?" asked Mary Anne. "Do they know how you feel?"

I sighed. "No. I mean, no, we haven't spoken to them, and no, they don't know how we feel."

"Why not?" asked Kristy sensibly.

"Because Mama and Daddy are so pleased to have Aunt Cecelia here. It solves all sorts of problems for them now that Mama's working. Also, they think they're making Aunt Cecelia happy. She's been so lonely since her husband died."

"But, Jessi," said Stacey, "Becca told me what you and she are doing to your aunt. Don't you think that talking to your parents would be a bit nicer than playing tricks on her?"

I could feel my face flush, especially as I explained to the other club members about the tricks. Then I added, "And that's another thing. Becca and I feel like we can't talk to Mama and Daddy *because* of the tricks. For some reason Aunt Dictator hasn't mentioned the tricks to our parents. It's as if they never happened. Becca and I are afraid that if we confront Mama and Daddy, Aunt Cecelia will tell on us. I'm completely stuck. I don't know what to do. And I *want* to talk to my parents, particularly because Aunt Cecelia really isn't a very good babysitter. She's doesn't play with Squirt. She does things for him that he should be learning to do for himself, and, I don't know, it's a big mess."

I felt miserable. I know I looked miserable. This was because Dawn said, "You look *so* miserable, Jessi."

"Boy," I replied. "If I have kids of my own, I'm *never* going to treat them the way

Aunt Dictator treats Becca and Squirt and me."

"Famous last words," said Kristy, laughing.

There was a pause, then we took some phone calls, and then, out of the blue, Mal said, "You know the five hundred-pound pancake? I wonder how they ever mixed the batter for it. In a cement-mixer?"

We left the meeting laughing.

11th CHAPTER

"Phoo! Phoo! Phee-*ew*! Jessi, when this volcano erupts, it is going to be the biggest mess." Jackie looked thrilled at the prospect.

There were just two days left until the science fair. The volcano had been built. The can inside it was filled with the chemicals, which we had been able to find, although Jackie and his mum had had to go to four different places before they found them.

"Jessi?" asked Jackie. I was sitting for him on another afternoon.

"Yeah?"

"Shouldn't we try the volcano just once? I mean, what if it doesn't work when the judges come around at the science fair?"

Although Jackie had a point, I had to tell him, "No. We can only let the volcano erupt once. Otherwise, you'll take a messy, gooey project to the fair. It won't be as impressive as if it erupts for the first time. Maybe we *should* test the chemicals, though. We could put them in another can, light them—*I* have to light the match, by the way—and make sure they really form the ash that's supposed to pour out of the crater. We'll test it in your drive and then wash the mess away with the garden hose."

"All *right!*" cried Jackie. "Oh, boy. A mess!"

Jackie and I carried the chemicals, an empty coffee can, and a packet of matches out to the drive. We followed the instructions for putting the chemicals in the can.

Then I said, "Okay, I'm going to toss a match in the can. By the way, Jackie, an adult will have to do that for you at the science fair, too. Me, your mum or dad, or one of the judges. Okay?"

"Okay."

"Now get ready. Stand back!"

Jackie ran to the edge of the drive. I lit a match, tossed it in the can, and ran. I turned around just in time to see ash spewing from the can and running down the sides. It was very realistic.

"Awesome!" exclaimed Jackie.

"It worked!" I cried.

Jackie ran to the can, but I stopped him. "Don't touch anything! The chemicals might burn your hands."

We turned on the hose, cleaned out the

can, and sprayed the ash down the drive and down a drain.

"Now," I said to Jackie, it's time to begin the final preparation of your project."

"Final preparation?" squeaked Jackie. "I thought we'd finished."

"Oh, no," I told him as we walked back into the house. "We have to work out how you're going to present your project. It needs a name. And you have to be able to tell the judges about it, not just have someone toss the match in and let the volcano erupt. How are you going to demonstrate your project?"

"Well," said Jackie, sounding sort of mixed up, "I'm not sure."

"All right. First, let's make a sign to label your volcano. What do you want to call your project?"

"I want to call it 'My Volcano'," said Jackie.

I shook my head.

"*The* volcano? *A* volcano?"

"No, no, no. It has to be much catchier," I told him.

We stood over the volcano in its glass box. "How about 'Welcome to the World of Volcanic Activity'?" I suggested proudly.

"Okay," agreed Jackie.

"You make the sign to hang in front of the volcano," I said. I handed Jackie a piece of paper and a Magic Marker.

Jackie worked laboriously for fifteen

minutes. Then he proudly held up a sign that looked like this:

Wellcom to the Wurld of
Vulcanice Acitivtie

"Jackie! No!" I exclaimed. "You've at least got to spell things right. You can't hang up a sign like that."

"But these are hard words. You have to help me."

"After all the studying we've done, you should know how to spell 'volcanic' and 'activity'," I said. "Here, *I'll* make the sign."

Jackie stared at the ground. And I thought, Boy, I have to do *all* the work. I even have to make the sign.

This is what I made:

Welcome to the World of
Volcanic Activity

"There. Now *that's* a sign," I told Jackie. I put it near his project. "What do you think of it?"

"Nice," he mumbled.

"Now, on to the next thing," I said enthusiastically.

"What next thing?" cried Jackie.

"We're heading over to Stoneybrook

Elementary to see where the science fair will be held. We've got to stake out the best spot for your project. Mal told me the judges walk around the main hall in a circle, starting at the front. I think your project should be one of the last they see. That way, they'll remember it when they're judging. Also, they'll be really impressed after all the goofy things they've looked at, like Barbie dolls on the moon."

Jackie didn't even ask what I was talking about. He just put on the sweater I handed him and followed me out of the back door and along the streets to the school.

"I hope the teachers are getting the hall ready for the fair," I said as we neared Stoneybrook Elementary.

"They are," said Jackie. "The hall was closed today."

"Good," I replied.

Jackie led me round to the back of the school, and we peeped through the windows of the main hall.

"There's Mr Peterson and Miss Handy. They're the caretakers," said Jackie. "It looks like they're putting desks in a big circle."

"I can see a banner," I pointed out. "Look, over the stage. Pretty good, huh?"

Stretched from one end of the hall to the other was a long paper banner that read: STONEYBROOK ELEMENTARY SCHOOL SCIENCE FAIR.

Jackie began to look excited. "And they're putting up pictures of dinosaurs and planets and birds and—and *every*thing on the walls!"

"Yeah!" I agreed. "Now let's see. What would be the best desk for you?" I looked and looked and finally decided on one. "That desk. Over there," I said, pointing. "It must be at the end of the judges' rounds. We've got to get here early, Jackie, so you can set up your project on that desk."

Jackie nodded distractedly, still looking in awe at the decorations. "The fair's important, isn't it?" he said. "I've never been to it before."

"It certainly is important. Think how you'll feel when you win. I wonder what your prize will be?"

"I don't care," said Jackie. "I just want to have the best project here. Then I can show Ian and John and Danny and all the boys in my class that I can do something really good. I bet *they*'ve never built a volcano."

"Probably not," I agreed.

We began to walk home. "Okay," I said. "Last thing. You've got two days to memorize what you're going to tell the judges about your project."

Jackie straightened his shoulders. "I'm going to say, 'This is my volcano. I built it myself. You light the chemicals and the ash goes *phoo, phoo, PHEW* out of the can!'"

"Oh, no, you're not. Jackie, this is a

science fair. You've got to explain how a volcano works. Remember the kinds of rocks we built our volcano on? Remember their names?"

"Iggus, morphus, and sedentary?"

I sighed. "Almost. Igneous, metamorphic, and sedimentary."

Jackie repeated the words fairly well.

"Okay, now what you want to say is that igneous rocks are born from fire, the molten rock that lies several miles below the surface of our earth. Above them are metamorphic rocks that have been changed by the heat . . ."

I finished my speech before we reached the Rodowskys'. I made Jackie start to memorize it. He wasn't bad. He stumbled on words a few times but he learned quickly.

When we'd been home for about twenty minutes, Jackie could spout off, "Igneous rocks are born from fire, the molten rock that lies several miles below the surface of the earth."

A while later, the speech was memorized.

"All right, hand signals."

"*Hand* signals?!"

"Yes."

"You mean as if I'm on my bike and I'm turning left and I stick out my left hand?"

"No. I suppose I meant to say 'hand *gestures*'."

"To impress the judges?"

Like I said, Jackie is a fast learner.

"You've got it," I told him. "See, I think you should even have a pointer. When you say, 'igneous rocks', point to the bottom layer of Plasticine. When you say, 'metamorphic rocks', point to the next layer, and so forth. Also, just as the chemicals are about to be lit—throw your hands in the air and say, 'the miracle of a volcano comes to life before our very eyes.' *Then* give your speech."

Jackie was grinning. He was going to get to put on a show.

"This'll be fun," he said, showing almost as much enthusiasm as when we'd set off the volcano in the drive.

When Mrs Rodowsky, Archie, and Shea came home, Jackie gleefully demonstrated his entire project—pointers, hand gestures, and all. I was late leaving for home, but I didn't mind. I was glad to see Jackie so happy.

12th CHAPTER

I might not have minded that I left the Rodowskys' a little late, but Aunt Dictator certainly did. She met me at our front door. I mean, she was just standing there waiting for me, arms crossed, mouth grim.

"You're late," she said.

(I was ten minutes late.) "I know, I'm sorry. Jackie was so excited about his volcano that I wanted—"

"When I'm in charge," Aunt Cecelia interrupted me (When isn't she in charge? I wondered), "you follow my rules. You are answerable to me. You must phone me if you're going to be late. Is that understood? *You must be responsible.* And part of being responsible is letting people know where you are."

Honestly, I thought. If I'd known I was going to be half an *hour* late, of course I would have phoned. But *ten minutes?* Mama and Daddy don't worry if I'm ten minutes late. They don't stand at doors with mental stopwatches going.

Aunt Cecelia had closed the door behind me and we were facing each other in the hall.

"Take off your coat," said Aunt Cecelia.

Obediently, I took it off.

"Aunt . . . Aunt Cecelia," I said. ("Aunt Dictator" had almost slipped out. I wondered if that would ever *really* happen.) "Mama and Daddy are strict with Becca and me. Squirt, too. But they're not . . . um . . ." (I almost said "not unreasonable") "I mean, they only get worried when they really need to. They wouldn't worry about ten minutes."

"Jessica, *I* am in charge. Late is late, whether it's two minutes, two hours, or two days." (That was a mean thing to say. She was referring to Becca getting stranded on the island, which she still claimed was my fault.)

"But honestly, Aunt Cecelia, Mama and Daddy really don't care about ten minutes. If I knew I was going to be much later, I would have phoned. I always do. Once I phoned home, and Mama said, 'Oh, Jessi. Thank you for letting us know—but we weren't even worried yet!' See, the rules here are that if—"

"I don't know how many times I have to tell you about the rules here, young lady.

They are mine when I'm in charge. End of story."

"Okay, okay, okay."

"Jessica! No answering back."

"That wasn't answering back!"

"It sounded like it."

"Well, it wasn't." I looked at my watch. "Uh-oh!" I grabbed my jacket back out of the cupboard. "I've got to go. I'm going to be late for the BSC meeting."

"*Oh*, no," said Aunt Cecelia. "You're not going to any meeting. Not today. Not after what you did."

"Because I was ten minutes late?!" I exclaimed. I couldn't believe it.

"Yes. Because you were late and you didn't phone me. You were irresponsible."

"Aunt Cecelia, don't you trust me? I'm not irresponsible. I can do things for myself. And I do the *right* things. If I were irresponsible I wouldn't have gone to Jackie's to babysit today. And missing a club meeting is very irresponsible. The other girls rely on me. We all rely on each other. We don't miss meetings unless we're ill or there's an emergency or something like a dance rehearsal comes up. When that happens, I let my friends know in advance. I can't just not go."

"Yes, you can. You're being punished. And if you carry on arguing, you won't be able to go to Friday's meeting, either."

My mouth hung open. I just stood there,

gazing at my aunt's angry face. Slowly the rest of the room came into focus—the clock on the chest, the open cupboard door, the boots on the floor of the cupboard, the striped wallpaper, and, standing in the doorway to the kitchen, Becca and Squirt. They were taking the scene in, and both looked frightened. Squirt was clinging to Becca's hand.

I think it was the sight of their scared faces that prompted me to do what I did next—defy Aunt Cecelia.

"You're not *really* in charge," I told her. "Maybe you're the sitter, but Mama and Daddy are in charge of our house, and I'm going to call them. If they say I can go to the meeting, then I can go. . . . And you can't stop me from calling," I added, dashing into the kitchen.

I reached the phone before Aunt Dictator could even open her mouth. First I phoned Daddy.

"Mr Ramsey's office," said his secretary.

"Oh, hi, Ed," I said, trying not to sound shaky or upset. "This is Jessi. Can I speak to my dad, please?"

"He's out of the office, Jess," Ed replied. (Ed is one of the few people who calls me Jess. I quite like it.) "Is this an emergency?"

I hesitated. "No," I said at last. Emergencies are fires and accidents and injuries. I wanted to talk to Daddy badly, but this was not an emergency and I didn't want to do anything *irresponsible*.

"Do you want me to tell your father you called?" asked Ed.

"That's okay. I'll see him at home tonight," I replied.

"Okay."

Ed and I hung up.

I glanced over my shoulder at Aunt Cecelia, who was watching me carefully. I turned around, picked up the phone again, and started to dial Mama's new work number. But halfway through, I stopped. Mama had said that, until she'd settled in to her job, Becca and I shouldn't call her at the office—unless there was an emergency and we couldn't get hold of Daddy.

Okay. No emergency, no call to Mama.

I hung up, defeated. Have you ever heard the saying, "Someone's got you over a barrel"? Well, Aunt Cecelia had me over a barrel. It meant that she'd put me in a situation I couldn't get out of. I had no options. In this case, I couldn't go to the BSC meeting. Not unless I just rode off, completely disobeying her. And that would make Mama and Daddy (not to mention Aunt Cecelia) very angry. I knew I couldn't go without talking to my parents first.

"Can I at least phone Kristy to tell her I won't be coming to the meeting?" I asked Aunt Dictator. "That *is* the responsible thing to do."

My aunt let me make the call.

"Hi, Kristy," I said. "Guess what? I'm really sorry, but Aunt Cecelia won't allow me to come to the meeting today. I was ten minutes late getting back from the Rodowskys' and she blew a fuse."

"Over ten minutes?"

"Yes. Can you believe it?"

"No. That's so unfair!"

"Listen, Kristy. Can you do something for me?" I lowered my voice even though I didn't need to. Aunt Dictator had taken Becca and Squirt into another room. "Can you phone me a lot during the meeting? It'll make it look as if you can't get along without me."

"Good idea!" replied Kristy. I knew she was smiling. That kind of thing appeals to her. "Your aunt'll think *you're* the BSC chairman!"

"Oh, thank you!" I told her.

Boy, did my friends live up to their promises. Our phone rang *fourteen* times between five-thirty and six o'clock.

By the third call, which was from Stacey, I whispered, "Aren't you lot tying up the club phone? I don't want to make you do that."

"No. We're using the Kishis' phone. We're taking turns going down to the kitchen and using the phone there," Stacey told me.

"Oh, okay." Then I raised my voice for

Aunt Cecelia's benefit. "No, tell Mrs Hobart I won't be able to sit then. I have a dance class that afternoon."

By 6:00, Aunt Cecelia had had it up to *here*. (Picture me holding my hand to my chin.) She couldn't believe all the phone calls, but there wasn't much she could do about them—except forbid me to attend another meeting, and she wouldn't do that again. Aunt Cecelia might be an old prune, but she's no fool.

After dinner that night, I just *casually* mentioned to Mama and Daddy that Aunt Cecelia and I were having some trouble, but I didn't make it sound like a big deal, so my parents didn't seem upset. They didn't even talk to Aunt Cecelia (at least, I don't think they did).

Aunt Cecelia and I were locked into an awful game now. I'd do something, she'd do something back, neither of us was happy— and Mama and Daddy hardly had any idea what was going on. They were too busy with their jobs and their grown-up lives.

That night, Aunt Dictator came into my room and announced, "We have *got* to do something about your hair." I suppose she was still annoyed about the fourteen phone calls.

Overbearing pig, I thought. I wanted to say those words to her face, but instead I said, "You can do whatever you want as long as Madame Noelle will approve."

Aunt Cecelia paused. For some reason, Mme Noelle is practically a goddess to my aunt. I suppose because I have come so far with my ballet—dancing lead roles and stuff.

Even so, Aunt Dictator was only slightly daunted. She got out a jar of cream, a brush, and some other things, and gave me the most awful hairdo possible. Fortunately, it was severe, so it was great for ballet. My hair would *never* be in my eyes. It couldn't escape the trap Aunt Cecelia had put it in.

"There," said my aunt. "Now you're someone I can be proud of."

Because of my *hair*?

I ran downstairs to complain to Mama and Daddy, but they were talking seriously about a problem Mama was having at work. They looked dead tired, too.

When they glanced up at me, standing in the doorway to the living room, all they said was, "Have you done something to your hair, Jessi?"

I left them alone. I didn't tell them what was really going on—that Aunt Cecelia was running our lives, and *ruining* mine.

13th CHAPTER

It was the evening of the science fair. I was so excited, you'd think *I'd* entered a project in it. (Well, in a way I had.) Anyway, the kids who were entering had to arrive at Stoneybrook Elementary by six-thirty in order to set up. The fair itself began at seven-thirty.

So at six-thirty, there were Stacey and Charlotte, Mal and Margo, Kristy and David Michael, Jackie and me, and a whole lot of kids and their parents or brothers or sisters or grandparents. Actually, Jackie and I had arrived at 6:20 to make sure we got our table sorted out.

Now, at nearly seven o'clock, the main hall was noisy and busy. All around Jackie and me were sighs of relief (when things went right) and groans (when things went wrong). Kids walked by carrying everything from huge pumpkins to complicated

103

electrical things. I could hear the sounds of gears turning, tools tinkering, and video equipment. The main hall was a pretty exciting place to be in.

"How do you feel, Jackie?" I asked him.

His volcano was loaded up and ready to explode. The "Welcome to the World of Volcanic Activity" sign was hung on the front of his desk. His pointer was in his hand.

"Fine," he replied, but he sounded nervous. "Listen to this: Igneous rocks are born from fire, the molting—"

"Molten," I corrected him.

"The molten rock that lies several feet—"

"Miles."

"Okay. Several miles below the surface of our wonderful earth."

"Just *our earth*, Jackie. Don't go over the top."

Jackie nodded miserably.

Seven-thirty. The main hall had really filled up. Teachers and parents and families and friends were pouring in.

"Look!" cried Jackie. "There are Mum and Dad and Archie and Shea!"

Boy, did Jackie seem relieved.

The Rodowskys made a beeline for The World of Volcanic Activity.

"Your project looks great, son," exclaimed Jackie's father.

"Yeah, it really does," Shea managed to admit.

"You know what?" I said. "I think I'm going to look around at the other projects before the judging begins. Jackie, you stay here and answer questions—but don't set the volcano off, okay?"

Jackie laughed. "Okay." He was beginning to feel pleased with himself. Even Shea hadn't seen the volcano explode. Jackie couldn't wait for the big moment. He wanted to prove something to Shea who, as his big brother, was always several steps ahead of him.

I walked slowly round the room, looking at the displays and experiments. I saw a model of a human heart made from Play-Doh (I think). I saw a small-scale "dinosaur war". I saw an impressive project about the Ice Age. I saw Charlotte's plants with her charts and graphs. One plant was considerably more healthy-looking than the other two, which were sort of scraggly.

"Which plant is that?" I asked, pointing to the full, green one.

"Guess," she said.

"The one that listened to classical music."

"Wrong." Charlotte grinned. "It's the Duran Duran plant. I'm not sure why. Maybe they were just really *fresh* seeds."

I laughed, and continued my walk through the exhibits. When I got back to Jackie's display, I found his family preparing to take a look around, so I said I'd stay with Jackie.

The volcano attracted a lot of attention.

"Hey! What's that?" asked a curly headed boy.

"A volcano," said Jackie proudly. "It can *erupt*. It makes ash and lava go everywhere. It's really messy."

"Can I see?" asked the boy.

Jackie's face fell. "Sorry. I can only make it explode once. I have to wait until the judges are here. You can see it then."

"Okay," said the boy, looking disappointed.

A few seconds later two girls walked past.

"A volcano!" exclaimed one. "Hey, I've always wondered. What *does* make a volcano?"

Jackie was prepared. "Igneous rocks are born from fire . . ." He said the entire speech without one mistake. I gave him the thumbs-up sign.

The girl frowned. "But *why*," she went on, "do igneous rocks do that? I mean, why does heat make a volcano erupt?"

Jackie was stumped. That wasn't part of his speech. And he couldn't demonstrate the volcano to the girls, either.

Just when I was beginning to feel guilty, my own family arrived. Well, Mama and Daddy and Becca did. Squirt was at home with Aunt Dictator. Becca had come because she wanted to see Charlotte's experiment, and my parents were there because of the volcano they'd been hearing about.

I began to feel better.

At eight o'clock, an announcement came over the PA system.

"Attention, please. May I have your attention? The judging will now begin. All participants in the science fair prepare to demonstrate and explain your projects to the judges. Visitors, please stand at the back of the room during the judging."

"That was our head teacher," Jackie informed me. (You'd have thought the President of the United States had just spoken.)

"Good luck, Jackie," I said. "I know you'll do fine. When it's time to make the volcano erupt, tell the judges you have to call me to light the match because you're not allowed to do that yourself."

Jackie swallowed and nodded. I joined my family at the back of the room.

The judging began.

Two women and a man walked solemnly from table to table. They looked each project over. They requested demonstrations. They asked questions.

Asked questions? Oh, no! Jackie couldn't talk about anything that wasn't in his speech. I hoped fervently that the judges would be so impressed with his demonstration that they wouldn't ask him any questions.

Tick, tick, tick. It was almost eight-thirty.

At last the judges reached The World of Volcanic Activity. I saw Jackie whisper something to one of the women. Then he saw me in the crowd and motioned for me to come forward. I did so, matches in hand.

"This," said Jackie as I reached his table, "is Jessi. She's my helper. She has to light the match for me."

(The judges smiled.)

I lit the match, told everyone to stand back, and tossed the match in the volcano. Jackie threw his hands in the air and cried, "The miracle of a volcano comes to life before our very eyes!"

PHOO! Lava was everywhere! It almost spattered the judges. Then it settled into a nice gooey flow down the sides of the volcano. The judges looked extremely impressed.

I stood at the side as Jackie made his speech, using the pointer.

The judges nodded and smiled.

And then the questions began.

"How," asked the man, "is the crater of a volcano created?"

"Um," said Jackie. He looked at me, but I couldn't help him. "Um," he said again. "I don't know." At least he didn't admit that I'd practically done the project for him.

"Well . . . what happens to the lava when it has flowed out of the crater?" asked one of the women.

"It—it's very hot . . ." Jackie said lamely.

I looked at the ground. This was my fault. I felt terrible as I watched the judges make notes on their pads of paper. They walked on to the last project of the fair without even telling Jackie, "Good work," or anything.

I went back to my parents and waited guiltily and nervously for the results of the fair to be announced.

"Jackie's project was great!" Dad said to me. "I've never seen such a thing. You really helped him."

A little too much, I thought.

Several minutes later, another announcement crackled over the loudspeaker. "The judges," said the principal, "have reached their decisions." (The judges were standing in the centre of the room.) "They have chosen first-, second-, and third-place winners. When the winners are announced, will they please receive their ribbons from the judges? Thank you." There was a pause. Then the principal continued. "Third prize goes to Charlotte Johanssen for her project entitled 'The Power of Music'."

Applause broke out. Charlotte, looking shy but pleased, edged over to the judges, received her yellow ribbon, and scurried back to her table, where she proudly attached the ribbon to the sign she'd made for her project.

The next two winners were announced. They went to kids I didn't know. I sought out Kristy, Mal, and my other friends in the crowd. Except for Stacey, they looked as disappointed as I felt.

But nobody looked more disappointed than Jackie, even though an Honourable Mention ribbon was already being fastened to his desk. (Every kid except the three winners was given an Honourable Mention.) The Rodowskys and I crowded around The World of Volcanic Activity.

"Don't be too upset, honey," Mrs Rodowsky told Jackie.

I had to speak up. "He has a right to be upset," I said.

Mr and Mrs Rodowsky turned to me. "Why?" they asked at the same time.

"Because—because I gave him so much help with his project that he really didn't do much of it himself."

"Yeah," said Jackie, giving me the evil eye.

"I'm really sorry," I went on. "I just wanted him to win. He's always saying he's no good at anything, or that he has bad luck. I wanted him to see that he *can* be a winner. I suppose I went about it all wrong, though."

Mr and Mrs Rodowsky were really nice. They understood what had happened. I got the feeling that they might have done things like this for Jackie in the past. Mr Rodowsky even admitted to building the glass and wood box for the volcano himself. (Well, with a *teeny* bit of help from Jackie.)

But Jackie, who's usually so easygoing and sunny, continued to scowl at me. "I just wanted to have fun," he said. "That was all. I just wanted to make a volcano erupt."

"Jackie, Jessi apologized to you," his father said gently.

"I know." Jackie finally managed a smile. But it quickly turned to a frown. "Oh, no," he muttered. "Here come John, Ian, and Danny. They're going to laugh at me. I just know it."

But the three boys who approached us looked excited.

"Jackie," said one, "your volcano was totally rad. Make it explode again!"

"Yeah," said another. "That was so cool."

Jackie explained why he couldn't "explode" the volcano again.

"Oh, well," said the boys. "It was still awesome." They started to walk away. "See you at school on Monday!" one called over his shoulder.

Jackie grinned at me like the Cheshire Cat. "I don't believe it!" he cried.

Mr and Mrs Rodowsky were smiling, too. "You know," said Jackie's mum, "there'll be another science fair next year. Jessi, maybe you could try helping Jackie again."

"I don't think so," I said. "I'd better not."

"Good," replied Jackie. "Because if I'm going to lose, I want to do it all by myself!"

We laughed, even Shea and Archie. But while I was laughing, I was thinking about something. I needed to talk to my parents. And I needed to talk to them badly.

14th CHAPTER

I left the Rodowskys and searched for my parents in the crowded main hall. I finally found them at Charlotte's table, along with Becca, Charlotte's parents, Stacey, and of course, Charlotte.

I pulled my mother aside. "Mama? Can we go home now?"

"What's the matter, darling? Don't you feel well?" Mama's hand immediately went to my forehead. "No temperature," she murmured.

"I feel fine," I told her. "I'm not ill. But I need to talk to you and Daddy. It's about Jackie and—and Aunt Cecelia and some other things. Please can we leave?"

"Of course we can." Mama looked alarmed.

We couldn't leave straight away, though. Saying goodbye took a while. Becca had to congratulate Charlotte one more time and

113

finger the prized yellow ribbon. Then I ran into Kristy.

"Sorry about Jackie," she said sincerely.

"Thanks," I replied. "Sorry about David Michael."

Kristy smiled. "Thank you. But it's funny—he doesn't seem upset at all."

At last my family had made our way out to our car. As we drove home, Mama said, "Becca, Jessi wants to have a talk about some things with Daddy and me, so when we get to our house, could you keep Squirt and Aunt Cecelia company for a while and let us have some privacy?"

"Okay." Becca sounded like she was on her way to the guillotine.

At home, Mama made tea, and she and Daddy and I sat at the kitchen table and sipped it.

"Now," said Mama, "tell us what's happened."

"Okay," I said, drawing in a breath. "It isn't something that's *just* happened; it's something that's been going on for a while. Only I didn't realize it—I mean, I didn't realize my part in it—until tonight, when Jackie didn't win a prize at the science fair."

My parents nodded, but they looked puzzled.

"See, this is what happened," I went on. "Jackie told me he thought it would be fun to build a volcano. He likes messy things. He also said the school science fair was

coming up. So I pushed him into entering.
. . . And then I did his whole project for
him."

"You what?" said Daddy.

"I did almost everything. I researched
volcanoes. I made him memorize that
speech. I even lettered the sign for his
project. It was as if I didn't trust him. I
treated him like a baby. I didn't listen to
him. I just forged ahead and did everything
my way, thinking it was better."

"Well, you certainly seem to have recog-
nized your faults," said Daddy.

"Did you apologize to the Rodowskys?"
asked Mama.

I nodded. "But that isn't all. See, there's
Aunt Cecelia, too. Becca and I," (I hadn't
planned to say this) "we call her Aunt
Dictator. She's running our lives. She
moved in here and she tells us what to do
and what not to do. Or she does things for
us. And she never listens to us and she
certainly doesn't trust us. Do you know that
she once wouldn't let me go to a BSC
meeting because I was ten minutes late
getting home and hadn't phoned her? I'd
have phoned if I was going to be later than
that—but not for ten minutes."

"Darling, why didn't you tell us about
that?" asked Mama.

"Well, I did try to call Daddy at work," I
admitted, "but Ed couldn't reach him. He
said you were out of the office, Daddy. And

then, well, Mama, I know your job is a big adjustment. I suppose I just didn't want to bother you with Aunt Cecelia problems. You neither, Daddy. She's your sister."

Mama and Daddy were silent for a moment. Then Daddy said, "I think it's time for a family conference."

(I knew he was going to say that.)

"Okay," I agreed. I guessed I could face Aunt Cecelia with Mama and Daddy and Becca around me.

Aunt Cecelia had just finished putting Squirt to bed, and she and Becca joined us in the kitchen. Mama poured tea for Aunt Cecelia and gave Becca a cup of orange juice.

Becca looked at me with eyes that were question marks.

"Cecelia," Daddy began, "it seems that Jessi hasn't been very happy lately. Nor has Becca. They feel . . . they feel that you don't trust them. They *are* big enough to do quite a few things on their own. We've been giving the girls a lot of responsibility. They're able to look after Squirt and to take care of themselves. But they think that you want to do things for them—things *they're* capable of doing."

Aunt Cecelia's face turned stiff. "Perhaps you don't need me, then?"

"Oh, yes, we do," Mama was quick to say. "The girls can't look after Squirt while they're at school, and—sorry, girls—but neither of them is much of a cook."

"I, um, I can understand how it happened," I spoke up. "I mean, why you took over, Aunt Cecelia. It's easy to do. I completely took over with Jackie and his volcano." (I had to tell the science-fair story again.) "But the thing was, I just wanted to show him that I care. I wanted him to feel good about himself."

"And *I* only wanted to show you that *I* care," Aunt Cecelia said. "I want you girls to grow up to be kind, responsible, neat, and polite. You know, it's an awful thing to have to say, but sometimes black people have to work twice as hard to prove themselves. It isn't fair, but that's the way it is—sometimes."

"That's sort of the way it is with Jackie, too," I said thoughtfully. "He's not stupid. He's clever. And he's kind and funny and a lot of other nice things. But he's a klutz, and that's how most people see him. So he has to work twice as hard to prove himself."

Silence. Then Aunt Cecelia, looking pained, said, "As long as we're baring our souls, I have to confess to something else. I was afraid I wouldn't be as good a sitter as you, Jessi."

"You *were*?" That was the last thing I'd expected to hear. "But you blamed *me* when Becca was stranded on the island."

"I know, but I shouldn't have. I needed something or someone to blame for that

117

tragedy, and you were it. But I know you've been taking care of your brother and sister—not to mention all the kids you sit for—for quite a while now, and you're an expert. I wasn't sure I could live up to you.

"On the other hand," Aunt Cecelia continued, her voice changing, growing stronger, "there's a little matter I need to mention to your parents. I think I've kept quiet about it long enough now, don't you?"

Dum da-dum dum. The practical jokes.

Becca and I nodded, but we couldn't look at anyone, not even at each other. We stared into our cups.

"What is it?" asked Daddy warily.

"Ever since I got here," Aunt Cecelia replied, "from the very beginning, I've found spiders—fake ones—in my bed, shaving cream in my shoes, and more, plenty more."

"*Girls,*" said Mama warningly.

"Well, we were angry. She was already taking over. She was our *babysitter*, ordering us about, making up rules. I don't need a sitter!" I cried. "I *am* a sitter. And a good one . . . like Aunt Cecelia said", I couldn't help pointing out. This time I looked directly at my aunt and held her gaze.

"Okay. Obviously we've got some problems to sort out," said Daddy. He turned to his sister. "Cecelia, I understand that you feel responsible for the girls, but they're used to certain things. For instance, Jessi never misses a meeting of the Babysitters Club. Not unless she has a special dance rehearsal or there's an emergency. We don't withhold that privilege as a punishment. I think that from now on, the girls should tell their mother or me about any plans they have. They can do this daily or weekly; we'll see what works best. We'll approve—or not approve—their plans, and then we'll tell you their schedules. Fair enough?"

"Fair enough," replied Aunt Cecelia. I could see her relax a little.

"Fair enough?" Daddy asked Becca and me.

"Yup," we agreed.

"Furthermore, the girls should be allowed to do the things we already trust them to do—do their own hair, choose their own clothes, that sort of thing," added Mama. "And perhaps," she went on, "it might be helpful if Cecelia is referred to simply as the children's *aunt*, not their sitter."

Aunt Cecelia smiled. "That sounds nice."

"Now," said Daddy, "there's a little matter of a punishment."

"A punishment?" squeaked Becca. "For who?"

"For *whom*," Aunt Cecelia corrected her gently.

"For you and your sister," Mama said sternly. "For spiders and shaving cream and I don't know what."

119

"Just a moment," interrupted my aunt. "Could I speak to you in private?" she asked my parents.

"Of course," they replied.

Becca and I escaped then. We didn't know what was going on, but we were glad to get out of there. That night, I slept like, well, like Squirt!

15th CHAPTER

Monday afternoon. Five-twenty-eight. Time for another BSC meeting.

We were all gathered. Kristy was sitting in the director's chair, visor on, pencil over her ear, watching Claud's digital clock, waiting for it to hit five-thirty on the dot.

Claudia was rummaging for junk food.

My friends and I were dressed in typical outfits. *Typical*, but not necessarily traditional. For instance, Stacey was wearing tight black trousers reaching just above her ankles, and sporting a column of four silvery buttons at the bottoms. (The buttons were just for decoration, I think.) Over the trousers she was wearing a *long* (past her knees) blue jacket made of soft material. Under that she was wearing a sleeveless blouse. Now that was unusual.

Claud was wearing a fake leopard-skin vest, a fairly tame blouse, and blue leggings.

She had made her jewellery herself—five papier-mâché bracelets that were painted in soft pastel colours.

Mary Anne and Dawn had swapped outfits, which they do pretty often. That's one nice thing about having a stepsister who's your best friend and also about your size. They were both dressed colourfully, and trendily, but not as wildly as Claud and Stace.

Then there was Kristy in her jeans and sweater. And finally Mal and me, also in jeans, but wearing (if I do say so myself) pretty *fresh* sweat shirts. And Mal had been allowed to buy high-top trainers with beaded designs on the sides!

Click. The clock turned to five-thirty.

"Order, please," said Kristy. "Treasurer, it's subs day."

Groan, groan, groan. We all produced our subs. Stacey counted the treasury money and looked pleased.

Before Kristy could even say, "Any club business?" the phone rang.

"Good sign!" she exclaimed, as Dawn answered it.

"Good afternoon, the Babysitters Club," said Dawn. Then, "Hi, Mrs Newton. . . . Friday? I'll check and phone you straight back."

We arranged that job as well as two others before things calmed down.

Then Mal said, "Did everyone survive the science fair?"

"Just barely," I replied.

"David Michael is ecstatic," reported Kristy.

"Over an Honourable Mention?" asked Dawn. "Anyone who didn't win got an Honourable Mention."

Kristy smiled. "I know. That doesn't matter to David Michael, though. He's just thrilled with the idea of a prize—any prize. He wouldn't even leave the ribbon on his project at the fair. He brought it home on Friday night, slept with it, and carried it around with him on Saturday until Watson suggested having it mounted. Now it's hanging over his bed. You'd think it was the Pulitzer Prize."

"That's sweet," said Mary Anne. "I'm glad David Michael is so happy. You know, it's funny what these fairs do for different kids."

"Yeah," said Mal. "Margo's proud of her project, but not the Honourable Mention. It doesn't mean much to her. She just wants everyone to see Barbie on the moon."

"What about Charlotte?" I asked Stacey.

Stacey rolled her eyes. "Oh, wow. You should see her. She's in science heaven. She found out that the names of the three winners will appear in the *Stoneybrook News*. She's got a huge boost of self-confidence."

"Jackie's reaction is a little different from everyone else's," I spoke up. "He doesn't care about the Honourable Mention, either. But once he got over being humiliated when he couldn't answer the judges' questions, he returned to his usual self. He doesn't want me to help him with next year's project, though."

"I don't blame him," said Kristy.

"Neither do I," I answered.

Then I told the BSC members what had happened on Friday night when my family and I had got home from the fair.

"What did your aunt want to talk to your parents about in private?" asked Claud.

"I have no idea. That was three days ago and I haven't heard a word about it. I'm afraid to ask."

"You don't think she's leaving, do you?" asked Mal suddenly.

I paused. Then I said, "Gosh. . . . I don't know. I thought we'd sorted everything out. We talked about how sometimes people take over when they just want to show they care. The way I did with Jackie and his project. And we laid down some rules. No. I don't think she's leaving."

You know what was weird? Just then, a little part of me *hoped* she wasn't leaving. If she did, what would we do about Squirt while Mama was at work? And who would be around to care *about* me (not for me) in the afternoons? The thought surprised me.

The phone rang then and we took a job call, and then another. When silence fell again, Dawn said, "Guess what? I'm going to California on our next school holiday. I'll get to see Dad and Jeff."

"That's *great*," said Kristy. "You know where Shannon Kilbourne is going?" (She paused dramatically.) "To Hawaii."

There was a huge chorus of "Oh, wows," and, "That is *so* fresh," and, "Boy, is she lucky."

Mal looked downcast. "I don't think I'll be going *any*where for a while. Dad's company is in trouble. He said he heard the chairman is going to lay off about half the people who work there. Dad says he thinks he'll be one of them."

"But he might not be," I pointed out.

"That's true. I suppose there's no point in worrying about it until it happens."

On that sombre note, the meeting broke up and I cycled home. I forgot about Mal and her father and his job, and began to feel cheerful. That was because this time I knew there would be no disapproving Aunt Cecelia waiting to pounce on me when I got home. There would be (I hoped) just an ordinary aunt who was probably making dinner and trying to entertain Squirt at the same time.

I was right on both counts.

When I entered our house I saw my aunt at the cooker, stirring things in pots. Sitting

125

at her feet was Squirt, who was banging frying pans with a wooden spoon and looking pretty pleased with himself.

"Hi, Aunt Cecelia," I was saying, just as Becca appeared next to me and gestured wildly but silently for me to follow her. So I did. I followed her upstairs to her room, where at last she found her voice—sort of.

"Jes—Jes—Look at—I mean, see what—"

"Becca, what on earth is the matter?" I asked her.

"Go and look at my slippers," was her reply.

I opened Becca's wardrobe door, turned on the light, bent down, and saw that her slippers were filled with shaving cream.

"I almost put them *on*," she said, horrified. "Then, I needed my torch, so I pulled back my bedspread" (Becca keeps her torch under her pillow) "and I found *this* in my bed." My sister held up a huge, disgusting plastic fly. "You didn't do these things, did you?" she asked, narrowing her eyes at me.

"Of course not," I replied. "I bet it was . . ."

"Aunt Cecelia!" we said together.

Then we bolted for my room. I found shaving cream in my slippers and a furry mouse (fake) under my pillow, and discovered that my bed was an apple-pie bed.

Becca and I just looked at each other.

Then we heard gentle laughter. We turned round. Aunt Cecelia was standing in my doorway, holding Squirt on her hip.

"I think we're even now," said my aunt.

I couldn't help smiling. "I suppose so."

"Yeah," agreed Becca.

"Aunt Cecelia . . . I'm sorry," I told her. "We weren't very nice to you. We didn't give you much of a chance."

"I didn't given you two much of a chance, either," she replied. "I did move in and take over. But that's going to change now."

"Hey, Aunt Cecelia, want to hear a joke?" asked Becca, which I knew was her way of apologizing.

"Of course I do. Come downstairs and tell it to me while I finish dinner. . . . Um, Jessi, you can watch Squirt for me."

"Thanks," I said.

So we returned to the kitchen and Becca told Aunt Cecelia a joke that I used to tell Becca.

"A long time ago, there was this Viking," Becca began. "And his name was Rudolph the Red. And one day he looked up at the sky and said to his wife, 'It's going to rain today.' And his wife said, 'No, it's not. The sky is blue and the sun is shining.' And Rudolph said, 'But it's still going to rain,' and his wife said, 'It's not,' and Ruldoph said, 'Is too.' So finally his wife said, 'How can you tell?' and her husband replied,

'Because Ruldoph the Red knows rain, dear.' "

Aunt Cecelia let out a burst of laughter like I'd never heard. Not from her, anyway. So we all began to laugh, even Squirt, although he hadn't understood the joke, of course.

And that was how Mama and Daddy found the four of us when they came home from work that night. All together in the kitchen, laughing.

"Well," said Daddy, "I think this household is finally settling down."

"Yup," I agreed. And I was pretty happy with the way things had turned out.

Later that night, I tore up the list of mean things to do to Aunt Cecelia.

GREEN WATCH by Anthony Masters

BATTLE FOR THE BADGERS

Tim's been sent to stay with his weird Uncle Seb and his two kids, Flower and Brian, who run Green Watch – an environmental pressure group. At first Tim thinks they're a bunch of cranks – but soon he finds himself battling to save badgers from extermination . . .

SAD SONG OF THE WHALE

Tim leaps at the chance to join Green Watch on an anti-whaling expedition. But soon, he and the other members of Green Watch, find themselves shipwrecked and fighting for their lives . . .

DOLPHIN'S REVENGE

The members of Green Watch are convinced that Sam Jefferson is mistreating his dolphins – but how can they prove it? Not only that, but they must save Loner, a wild dolphin, from captivity . . .

MONSTERS ON THE BEACH

The Green Watch team is called to investigate a suspected radiation leak. Teddy McCormack claims to have seen mutated crabs and sea-plants, but there's no proof, and Green Watch don't know whether he's crazy or there's been a cover-up . . .

GORILLA MOUNTAIN

Tim, Brian and Flower fly to Africa to meet the Bests, who are protecting gorillas from poachers. But they are ambushed and Alison Best is kidnapped. It is up to them to rescue her *and* save the gorillas . . .

SPIRIT OF THE CONDOR

Green Watch has gone to California on a surfing holiday – but not for long! Someone is trying to kill the Californian Condor, the bird cherished by an Indian tribe – the Daiku – and without which the tribe will die. Green Watch must struggle to save both the Condor and the Daiku . . .

THE UNDERWORLD TRILOGY
Peter Beere

When life became impossible for the homeless of London many left the streets to live beneath the earth. They made their homes in the corridors and caves of the Underground. They gave their home a name. They called it UNDERWORLD.

UNDERWORLD

It was hard for Sarah to remember how long she'd been down there, but it sometimes seemed like forever. It was hard to remember a life on the outside. It was hard to remember the real world. Now it seemed that there was nothing but creeping on through the darkness, there was nothing but whispering and secrecy.

And in the darkness lay a man who was waiting to kill her . . .

UNDERWORLD II

"Tracey," she called quietly. No one answered. There was only the dark threatening void which forms Underworld. It's a place people can get lost in, people can disappear in. It's not a place for young girls whose big sisters have deserted them. Mandy didn't know what to do. She didn't know what had swept her sister and her friends from Underworld. All she knew was that Tracey had gone off and left her on her own.

UNDERWORLD III

Whose idea was it? Emma didn't know and now it didn't matter anyway. It was probably Adam who had said, "Let's go down and look round the Underground." It was something to tell their friends about, something new to try. To boast that they had been inside the secret Underworld, a place no one talked about, but everyone knew was there.

It had all seemed like a great adventure, until they found the gun . . .

Also by Peter Beere

CROSSFIRE
When Maggie runs away from Ireland, she finds herself
roaming the streets of London destitute and alone. But
Maggie has more to fear then the life of a runaway. Her
step-father is an important member of the IRA – and if he
doesn't find her before his enemies do, Maggie might just
find herself caught up in the crossfire . . .

MYSTERY THRILLERS

THE SONG OF THE DEAD by Anthony Masters
For the first time in years "the song of the dead" is heard around Whitstable. Is it really the cries of dead sailors? Or is it something more sinister? Barney Hampton is determined to get to the bottom of the mystery . . .

THE FERRYMAN'S SON by Ian Strachan
Rob is convinced that Drewe and Miles are up to no good. Where do they go on their night cruises? And why does Kimberley go with them? When Kimberley disappears Rob finds himself embroiled in a web of deadly intrigue . . .

TREASURE OF GREY MANOR by Terry Deary
When Jamie Williams and Trish Grey join forces for a school history project, they unearth much more than they bargain for! The diary of the long-dead Marie Grey hints at the existence of hidden treasure. But Jamie and Trish aren't the only ones interested in the treasure – and some people don't mind playing dirty . . .

THE FOGGIEST by Dave Belbin
As Rachel and Matt Gunn move into their new home, a strange fog descends over the country. Then Rachel and Matt's father disappears from his job at the weather station, and they discover the sinister truth behind the fog . . .

BLUE MURDER by Jay Kelso
One foggy night Mack McBride is walking along the pier when he hears a scream and a splash. Convinced that a murder has been committed he decides to investigate and finds himself in more trouble than he ever dreamed of . . .

DEAD MAN'S SECRET by Linda Allen
After Annabel's Uncle Nick is killed in a rock-climbing accident, she becomes caught up in a nerve-wracking chain of events. Helped by her friends Simon and Julie, she discovers Uncle Nick was involved in some very unscrupulous activities . . .

CROSSFIRE by Peter Beere
After running away from Southern Ireland Maggie finds herself roaming the streets of London destitute and alone. To make matters worse, her step-father is an important member of the IRA – if he doesn't find her before his enemies do, she might just find herself caught up in the crossfire . . .

THE THIRD DRAGON by Garry Kilworth
Following the massacre at Tiananmen Square, Xu flees to Hong Kong, where he is befriended by John Tenniel, and his two friends Peter and Jenny. They hide him in a hillside cave, but soon find themselves swept up in a hazardous adventure that could have deadly results . . .

VANISHING POINT by Anthony Masters
In a strange dream, Danny sees his father's train vanishing into a tunnel, never to be seen again. When Danny's father really does disappear, Danny and his friend Laura are drawn into a criminal world, far more deadly than they could ever have imagined . . .

Mother's Helper
The Cheerleader
by A. Bates

The Return of the Vampire
by Caroline B. Cooney

April Fools
The Lifeguard
Teacher's Pet
Trick or Treat
by Richie Tankersley Cusick

My Secret Admirer
by Carol Ellis

Funhouse
The Accident
The Invitation
by Diane Hoh

Thirteen
by Christopher Pike, R.L. Stine and others

Beach Party
The Baby-sitter
The Baby-sitter II
The Boyfriend
The Snowman
The Girlfriend
by R.L. Stine

The Waitress
by Sinclair Smith

Look out for:

The Window
by Carol Ellis

The Fever
by Diane Hoh

Hit and Run
by R.L. Stine

The Train
by Diane Hoh

Beach House
by R.L. Stine

The Perfume
by Caroline B. Cooney

The Ripper
by Diane Hoh

THE BABYSITTERS CLUB

Need a babysitter? Then call the Babysitters Club. Kristy Thomas and her friends are all experienced sitters. They can tackle any job from rampaging toddlers to a pandemonium of pets. To find out all about them, read on!

No 1: **Kristy's Great Idea**
No 2: **Claudia and the Phantom Phone Calls**
No 3: **The Truth About Stacey**
No 4: **Mary Anne Saves The Day**
No 5: **Dawn and the Impossible Three**
No 6: **Kristy's Big Day**
No 7: **Claudia and Mean Janine**
No 8: **Boy-Crazy Stacey**
No 9: **The Ghost at Dawn's House**
No 10: **Logan Likes Mary Anne!**
No 11: **Kristy and the Snobs**
No 12: **Claudia and the New Girl**
No 13: **Goodbye Stacey, Goodbye**
No 14: **Hello, Mallory**
No 15: **Little Miss Stoneybrook . . . and Dawn**
No 16: **Jessi's Secret Language**
No 17: **Mary Anne's Bad-Luck Mystery**
No 18: **Stacey's Mistake**
No 19: **Claudia and the Bad Joke**
No 20: **Kristy and the Walking Disaster**
No 21: **Mallory and the Trouble with Twins**
No 22: **Jessi Ramsey, Pet-sitter**
No 23: **Dawn on the Coast**
No 24: **Kristy and the Mother's Day Surprise**
No 25: **Mary Anne and the Search for Tigger**
No 26: **Claudia and the Sad Goodbye**
No 27: **Jessi and the Superbrat**
No 28: **Welcome Back, Stacey!**
No 29: **Mallory and the Mystery Diary**
No 30: **Mary Anne and the Great Romance**
No 31: **Dawn's Wicked Stepsister**
No 32: **Kristy and the Secret of Susan**
No 33: **Claudia and the Great Search**
No 34: **Mary Anne and Too Many Boys**

No 35: **Stacey and the Mystery of Stoneybrook**
No 36: **Jessi's Babysitter**

Look out for:

No 37: **Dawn and the Older Boy**
No 38: **Kristy's Mystery Admirer**
No 39: **Poor Mallory!**
No 40: **Claudia and the Middle School Mystery**

BABYSITTERS LITTLE SISTER

Meet Karen Brewer, aged 6. Already known to Babysitters fans as Kristy's little sister, for the very first time she features in a series of her very own.

No 1: **Karen's Witch**
No 2: **Karen's Roller Skates**
No 3: **Karen's Worst Day**
No 4: **Karen's Kittycat Club**
No 5: **Karen's School Picture**
No 6: **Karen's Little Sister**
No 7: **Karen's Birthday**
No 8: **Karen's Haircut**
No 9: **Karen's Sleepover**
No 10: **Karen's Grandmothers**
No 11: **Karen's Prize**
No 12: **Karen's Ghost**
No 13: **Karen's Surprise**
No 14: **Karen's New Year**
No 15: **Karen's in Love**